The Sound of the Sea

A FIVE ISLAND COVE NOVEL

SAIL AWAY
BOOK TWO

JESSIE NEWTON

ISBN-13: 978-1-63876-199-0

Praise for Jessie Newton

★★★★★ *"On the pedestal with Wendy Wax and Inglath Cooper." ~ Amazon reviewer, on The Lighthouse (Five Island Cove, Book 1)*

★★★★★ *"This is a series to take you away from the day's stress. You will find comfort in the strength of each of these women. They support each other in friendships we all dream of having. There is drama, there is laughter, there is family, there is a human connectedness." ~Nook Reviewer, on The Lighthouse (Five Island Cove, Book 1)*

★★★★ *"A thought-provoking novel of relatable friendships. Jessie Newton giftedly reveals each woman's past and current life, bringing them to life in a way that allows them closure and a new beginning." ~InD'Tale Magazine, on The Lighthouse (Five Island Cove, Book 1)*

For those of you who find yourself on wide open water, in the taste of the tropics, or in the sound of the sea - the way I do.

Chapter One

Jennifer Golden sat at her vanity, the oval mirror showing her a woman with a pretty smile. She wore no makeup, but she'd never needed much. Now that she'd passed sixty-five, Jennifer could definitely see the lines around her eyes and in her forehead far easier than before.

It had happened overnight too, it seemed. She was young and beautiful one day, and the next, she'd aged well, and she now considered herself a senior and still beautiful.

She dabbed cream onto her middle and fourth fingers and began to swirl it gently around her face. Her thoughts did the same, but in a much more violent way.

She'd messed everything up with her daughter, Robin. Again.

Honestly, the skill with which Jennifer did that should be taught in seminars and courses worldwide. A sigh fluttered between her lips, and she finally stood from the stool and flipped off the light surrounding the mirror.

Everything in her life looked put together and seamless. From the outside. Even from inside her quaint, cozy cottage near the sea, Jennifer made sure everything had a place and everything was kept in that exact place.

The turmoil existed inside her. She wasn't sure how she'd made it to almost seventy and still cared so much about what others thought of her. Of what the neighbors might think if she didn't clip her grass precisely when it needed to be done, or what they might say if she left her garbage can out overnight instead of bringing it in the same day it got emptied.

Exhaustion pulled through her and on her as she settled into bed, because even that had to be perfect. She closed her eyes and breathed in deep. She counted as she told herself to expand her belly, then her ribs, then her throat as she continued to take air in and in and in.

She held the breath for a moment, and all she could think was *melt* as she exhaled the day away. Her therapist had taught her to "melt into the table" during a massage, and not for the first time, Jennifer wondered if she should go see a different type of therapist.

One who could help her untangle the knots in her heart and mind, and not only the ones in her shoulders and neck.

She did indeed melt into the mattress, imagining the strength of it as it held her up in space and time, denying gravity the opportunity to drag her as far down as she'd go. Her neck relaxed, then her shoulders, and her back. Her hips and her legs, and finally, her arms as she curled them around a pillow.

But her mind would not shut off, as she had a lunch date with her daughter tomorrow, and Jennifer had some news she had to share before too much more time passed.

"She already knows," she murmured to herself, and that reassurance, weak as it might have been, allowed her to finally let her mind melt into slumber too.

THE FOLLOWING DAY, JENNIFER WORKED AT DR. Benson's office the way she normally did on Tuesday mornings. She worked all day Wednesday and then again on Thursday morning, and then she had four days off. That was when she went through the numerous holdings she'd inherited from her husband, planned her business phone calls, or daydreamed about the perfect family holiday, with candied ham and scalloped potatoes in the center of the table. All of her children and grandchildren would be gathered around, and everything would smell like pine trees and cinnamon.

She swallowed as she waited at the table inside The Glass Dolphin. She loved this new addition to Five Island Cove, and despite Robin's protests that it was too fancy and too costly for her, she'd agreed to meet there.

Jennifer would offer to pay; Robin would decline.

Even if she couldn't afford The Glass Dolphin, she would not allow Jennifer to do anything charitable for her.

Regret lanced through her, but she lifted her chin high. Robin and Duke had been through several storms in their married life—literally and figuratively—and Jennifer believed they'd grown closer as they'd relied on each other. She and Connor, her deceased husband, had not wanted to interfere with the children and their affairs once they became adults.

"I wish you were here," she whispered to herself, thinking of the man she'd lost so early in life. Connor had only been fifty-two when pancreatic cancer had taken him. Robin had been thirty, and Stuart, her youngest child, only twenty-seven.

They missed their father, Jennifer knew, because he'd been the emotional one. The one they went to when they needed help with their homework, another student at school...or Jennifer herself. He'd been ruthless when it came to business, but none of that had transferred to the way he cared for their children.

Without him, Jennifer had done a poor job of making sure Stu and Robin knew how much she loved them. She was either too overbearing and drove them away, or too cold and callous, which also drove them away.

Her hand trembled as she reached for her wine glass and took a sip. Robin was late. Jennifer couldn't help a slip of impatience for her daughter as it swept through her. Jennifer loathed it when people were late, as if her time wasn't as important as theirs.

She gently reminded herself that she'd been late a time or two in her life, and no one could be expected to be perfect all the time. The truth was, Robin was probably sitting outside in the parking lot, or on a bench down the boardwalk, psyching herself up enough to come inside for this lunch. They hadn't been on the best of speaking terms for months now, since she'd discovered that Jennifer had tried to silently invest in Friendship Inn.

She'd asked questions about Jennifer's finances—that Jennifer had refused to answer. She saw now that a door from heaven had been opened up wide, and she'd failed to walk through it. She felt like she had to chip away at cement now, without seam or crevice, to talk to her daughter.

She waited another ten minutes, then twenty. Robin didn't appear and she didn't text. Impatience ate away at Jennifer, who finally looked at her phone. With a rush of adrenaline that quickly morphed into horror, she realized she'd had the device on silent.

Robin had called—three times. She'd texted twice that many.

Mom, I'm so sorry, but I can't make lunch. Maybe you haven't left yet. Something's come up in the city, and Duke and I are on the way there to see what we can do to help Mandie.

Odd that you're not answering... Maybe you're in that dead zone by the orchids.

No emergency in the city. Mandie just got hit by a bicyclist. Duke's staying here with Jamie. I'm going to make sure she's okay.

Jennifer tapped to call Robin, whose texts and calls were only about a half an hour old. "Mom," her daughter said, her voice tight and rushed. "There you are."

"I'm sorry," she said, words that very rarely left her mouth. "I had my phone in my purse, and it was on silent. I didn't realize, and I never heard it chirp."

"That's what silent means," Robin said. Commotion and chaos sounded on her end of the line. "I have to go. Stu's only twenty minutes from the hospital, so he'll know more than me. Call him for more details. I'll catch you up later."

The call ended, and Jennifer looked down at her device. Sadness and disappointment cut through her, the same way Robin's words from last year had.

She couldn't call Stuart, for he currently wasn't talking to her.

"Are you ready to order?" a young woman asked, and Jennifer looked up at her.

She immediately shook away all of the negative. Never mind that her daughter didn't need her. Or that her son wouldn't speak to her. Both of those things were her fault anyway. "Yes," she said smoothly. "I'd love the lobster-stuffed blue crab, please." She lifted her wine glass. "And another glass of this."

"Yes, ma'am." The young woman left, and Jennifer looked out the wide expanse of windows. All she wanted was to get away. Get away from this restaurant. Lose herself in the sound of the sea. Have only the wide, blue sky overhead. The scent of the salt, and the call of the gulls as they raced alongside a ship.

"A ship," she whispered. She'd taken holiday cruises for the past two years, and her heartbeat did a jump and a bump inside her chest. Could she find a cruise line that wasn't booked for the holidays?

She'd recently cruised with Grand Adventure and then High Caribbean, but all of their Christmas cruises were booked. Telephone numbers sat at the top of the screen, and she could call and try to get a last-minute cancellation or be put on a waiting list.

She didn't want to do either of those. There had to be dozens of cruise lines in the world, and Jennifer had more money than she could ever spend. While she waited for her fancy lunch to arrive, while life in the cove moved around her, her thumbs flew across her screen.

She typed in *best cruise for single women over sixty*, and the list that populated took less time than it took for her to breathe to appear on her screen. She scanned the list, her eyes catching on the words "luxury" and "voted best cruise line for singles for ten years running" under one bolded listing.

After tapping there, a gorgeous website bloomed to life, and Jennifer's breath caught in her throat. The Silver Sails cruise line was immaculate. They touted themselves as the premier vacation for anyone in the prime of their life, with private suites, all of which had balconies, huge buffets, and nightly entertainment.

Two requirements looped at the top of the page, and Jennifer read them out loud. "Are you single? Over sixty? Then our luxury yacht is for you."

"Here you go," the waitress said, and Jennifer jerked her eyes up as the plate of food got set down. The crab looked buttery and delicious, with chunks of real lobster meat spilling from the insides. "Can I get you anything else right now?"

Some sanity, Jennifer thought. She painted a perfect smile on her face. "No, thank you, dear."

The waitress left, and instead of immediately diving into her lunch, though it smelled rich and salty and delicious, Jennifer went right back to her phone. Surely a cruise line like this wouldn't have any availability in only two weeks. She tapped anyway, her finger trembling for an entirely different reason now.

Spend Christmas on the open sea! it read at the top of the page. *Still booking for our longest, highest-rated cruise for singles over sixty.*

Jennifer needed this escape. She *craved* it. Perhaps away from the cove, away from the tension with her daughter and the silence from her son, she'd be able to work out what to do with the warped and broken relationships in her life.

Perhaps the ship *Sweet Sea Dreams* would have all the answers for her.

She shook her head, the practical side of her roaring back to life. A yacht couldn't mend years of harsh words and hurt feelings, and Jennifer knew it.

Still, she tapped, and typed, and before she even took a single bite of her lunch, she'd booked herself a luxury, fifteen-day cruise aboard the *Sweet Sea Dreams*. Now, she could only pray that leaving the cove for the third Christmas in a row wouldn't add more wedges between her and Robin...right when Jennifer was trying to figure out how to get rid of them.

Chapter Two

Jennifer rose to her feet and tucked her phone into her purse. The busyness of the airport drove her to the brink of insanity, especially around the holidays, and she couldn't wait for the more relaxed atmosphere of the ship.

"Yacht," she whispered to herself. She'd just finished texting Robin all the details of her holiday vacation, and Robin had brought up the fact that she'd be going through the Panama Canal with less than ten feet to spare on either side of the yacht.

I didn't realize it was such a small vessel, Robin had said. *You sure you're safe?*

Jennifer had told her that her husband went out onto the churning, foaming ocean on a fishing vessel not much smaller than the luxury yacht, and Robin had dropped the subject. If they'd been together in person, Jennifer felt certain her daughter would've been wearing her mouth in a tight, grim line while she held her silence.

She sighed as she shouldered her tote bag and headed for the line to board the plane. She didn't mean to ruffle Robin's feathers. Yes, this was her first time on this cruise line. She'd never been on a ship this small before. She'd never done a singles cruise before either, and Jennifer's stomach already rumbled with nerves. She couldn't handle her daughter's questions too.

She'd be gone from Five Island Cove for the next seventeen days. A day of travel to San Diego, where she'd board her luxury yacht tomorrow morning. Every suite was made for a single person—obviously—and there were only one hundred suites on-board the yacht. Every one had a balcony of some size, and since Jennifer had booked so late, hers was on the upper end of the pricing. Thus, her balcony was one of the largest on the yacht. She wasn't sure what floor she'd be on yet, but the type of room she'd booked indicated that she'd be on the second, third, or fourth levels.

The plane took off, and Jennifer relaxed into the seat. Her mind drifted, and while she'd brought her laptop and could do some work while she flew or sailed, she also wanted a vacation—a true vacation—deep in her bones.

Since Connor's death, Jennifer had been handling everything. Things she hadn't even known she needed to handle. Things she'd had to learn from scratch. Things she'd rather someone else handle.

She'd put her trust and faith in a financial advisor

several years ago, and after a huge five-figure loss, she'd learned the hard way to manage her own wealth. It was a big job, and one she paid close attention to. For a while there, it had almost become an obsession for her.

Jennifer had found a healthier balance now, but she still liked to check on things often. She wasn't one who bought and sold stocks or bonds daily. She liked to watch the market, and she liked to invest in stable things that would pay out in three to five years. At her age, that made the most sense.

She opened her eyes as the flight attendant asked for her drink order. "I'll have a white wine, please," she said. She'd booked a flight as direct as possible, but she had to change planes in Minneapolis. Then she'd have one more flight that would get her the rest of the way to California.

No matter what, one glass of wine wouldn't make her tipsy enough to miss her connection.

About the time her second flight taxied down the runway, Jennifer acknowledged to herself that she needed to clue Robin into her financial situation. Her daughter had asked about it a few months ago, but Jennifer hadn't liked the circumstances under which the topic had come up.

Robin knew where the living will and Jennifer's estate binder waited for her once Jennifer passed—she'd double-checked with her again before taking this trip. But her daughter would be ten times as overwhelmed with what she'd find inside all of Jennifer's accounts as Jennifer had been after Connor's passing.

If Jennifer could sit down with Robin and show her around, the transition would go far better and be way less shocking.

Jennifer swallowed and nodded to the flight attendant offering headphones on this leg of the journey. She took the headphones and plugged them into the screen on the back of the seat in front of her. She needed an escape, and as she put on a blaring, loud movie, she told herself *Soon.*

She'd tell Robin about the many and varied accounts she held—and which her daughter stood to inherit —soon.

THE FOLLOWING MORNING, JENNIFER ENTERED A small, seaside building that didn't look anything like the home of a luxury cruise line. She'd taken cruises out of Miami and Galveston in the past couple of years, but those ships were absolutely huge, and she'd gone down to the docks to board them.

This nondescript, almost falling-down building looked like she'd buy bait for a trip out on the ocean, not board a yacht that likely cost over six-figures. However, an array of people with plenty of luggage stood inside the building, and Jennifer wheeled her single suitcase over the lip on the floor and inside, looking for a place to join a line.

Dividers marked a path up to the counter, where half

a dozen people worked. Jennifer joined the line, smiling benignly to the woman in front of her. She knew she'd booked a singles cruise, but she wasn't ready to start mixing and mingling yet.

The yacht would depart in a couple of hours, and Jennifer couldn't wait to change out of her traveling clothes, unpack her bag in her suite, and find the first restaurant that would give her a glass of white wine and a bowl of Cocoa Pebbles with real cream. She had a real weakness for the sugary cereal, and it was never Christmas without a bowl of the chocolatey breakfast treat.

The line inched at times and moved full steps at others. Jennifer finally checked in, and a personal valet took her suitcase with a smile a mile wide.

"We'll have your bag waiting for you in your room," the woman behind the computer said. "I've got you...in room...three-twenty-five." She looked up, her eyes bright and blue and filled with light. "It's a lovely room. An amazing balcony off the back that's as big as the interior rooms."

She slid something across the counter to Jennifer. "The weather is absolutely perfect for the next two weeks, only turning a bit colder and stormier as the yacht rounds the Florida keys and heads back up to New York City." She beamed at this obviously great news. "Where are you coming to us from?"

"Near New York City," Jennifer said with a smile. "It

is very cold there." She took the papers, which she'd go through in the privacy of her suite.

"Well, I hope you enjoy your time aboard *Sweet Sea Dreams*," the woman said. "We'll begin boarding in about twenty minutes." She indicated an area to Jennifer's left. "The waiting area is right over there. Our Activities Director is already beginning our singles activities."

Jennifer glanced to the left, her stomach doing a swoop. Was she ready to start talking to the other people she'd spend the next fifteen days with? With only one hundred of them, she'd surely have time to meet them all.

She swallowed and looked back at the woman. She gave her a tight smile, tucked the papers away, and moved to the left. She'd put her purse inside her tote, and those things never went anywhere without her. She could survive without clothes or toiletries for a few days, as long as she had her money and her computer.

Hovering on the edge of the assembled crowd, Jennifer was content to observe for several minutes. No one approached her, and she made no move to enter the fray of people. Some of them obviously knew one another; they'd come on this trip together. A trio of women her age, all of them sipping flutes of champagne and glancing around like they were in their twenties, looking for their next date.

Men would rotate over to them and then away, none of them staying for longer than a few minutes. She didn't see groups of men who'd come together, but she did see mixed-gender pairs, and she wondered if they were friends or siblings.

Before she knew it, a man's voice came over the public address system. "Ladies and gentleman, we'll begin boarding in about five minutes. Please have your ticket and your passport, as we have to check both before we let you onto the yacht. We'll be boarding our luxury line passengers first, and then moving from the back of the ship to the front."

Jennifer had been on cruises before, but it took hours and hours to load one of those. With only one hundred people, this would take less time than it had for Jennifer to get on the two planes that had brought her here.

She wasn't a luxury liner, but she would be boarding near the front of the group, as her room was at the back of the ship. Anxiety ran through her, because she couldn't hide out in her room for the next two weeks. She couldn't simply ignore the other ninety-nine people about to embark on this journey with her.

Perhaps for a few more minutes. Just enough time for her to feel more settled. To actually be physically settled. She edged forward, thinking she'd simply take up a position a little closer to the door that had just opened, when someone said her name.

She turned toward the woman, not immediately recognizing her. A woman and a man stood there, both of them clearly in their late sixties, the same as Jennifer. They'd both had blonde hair at one point, with the man's darker than the woman's, and Jennifer recognized the similarities between them and classified them as siblings in only a blink of time. Crinkly blue eyes. A straight, sloped nose. Pointed chin. The woman had high cheekbones, while the man's ears had continued to grow, as they did.

They both had straight white teeth, and they looked at one another and then back to Jennifer simultaneously.

"It is you." The woman with whitening golden hair grinned and started dancing on her tip-toes. "It is her. Mitch, look at her!"

The other woman lifted both hands above her head, her giggle turning into a screech that had everyone in the immediate area turning toward the three of them. The woman launched herself toward Jennifer, who had no choice but to catch her lest they both fall down.

"Blanche," Mitch said, and with that single syllable, memories flooded Jennifer's mind.

"Blanche?" she repeated. New warmth moved through her, filling her with laughter. She knew the woman now—Blanche Gibb. Her old college roommate from many, many years ago.

They laughed together, and Jennifer hugged her tightly before she pulled back. With her hands on Blanche's shoulders, she peered at her. "What in the world are you doing here?" She looked over to Mitch, a man she'd only met a few times, decades ago.

A good air emanated from him, and Jennifer couldn't help the instant shyness that overcame her. She ducked her head, her own golden hair barely brushing her chin. Blanche wore hers shorter, though she'd always had a bit of eccentricity when it came to her hairstyles.

"Taking a cruise, of course." Blanche grinned and grinned. All at once, her smile faltered and fell from her face. She stepped back, leaving Jennifer reeling a little bit at how quickly her friend's emotions had changed.

With another lightning-fast switch, like she'd flipped on a light, Blanche brightened again and spun to Mitch. "Do you remember my brother? Mitchell?"

"We met only a few times." Still, his smile remained bright and hopeful as he stepped forward, hand extended.

Jennifer put her hand in his, a sizzle in her blood she hadn't felt in a while. Her smile met his, and he nodded. It couldn't be an acknowledgement of the attraction fizzling between them. Could it?

No matter what, Jennifer suddenly held a brighter outlook for this cruise than she had five minutes ago.

"Great to see you again," she said.

"You too." He pulled his hand back.

"We need to meet up on the yacht," Blanche said, her enthusiasm something that hadn't dimmed. She linked her arm through Jennifer's. "For lunch."

Jennifer loved good food and good company, and she'd enjoyed living with Blanche Gibb. "Absolutely," she said. "We'll get settled, and then we'll meet up for lunch."

Chapter Three

Blanche Gibb-Hanson held her phone against the keypad of her suite, her cheeks aching for how much she'd been smiling. Thankfully, Mitch's cabin sat down the hall, and he'd gone inside after saying, "See you in a half-hour, Blanche."

The weight of the past nine months settled on her shoulders as she passed from the hallway to her suite. The door very nearly cut off her foot it slammed so quickly and so hard, but Blanche managed to dance out of the way. She twisted the lock, drew a deep breath, and faced the cabin.

A small bathroom sat to her right, with a king-sized bed past that. Luxury linens clothed it, and Blanche couldn't wait to flop into the array of cushy pillows and cottony blankets. However, at her age, she knew once she collapsed into that bed, she'd be taking a nap instead of meeting her friend for lunch.

Therefore, she went by the bed, noting that her funky, tie-dyed suitcase had been set up onto a luggage rack, and toward the wide wall of windows in front of her. Her suite's balcony pushed out onto the side of the ship, not the back, and Blanche took a deep breath as she exited the room through the double doors.

"That room needs to be aired out," she said to the lapping water. She did leave the door open behind her, and she gripped the railing and looked into the distance. The yacht hadn't left the dock yet, though she and Mitch had been two of the last passengers onboard.

She expected they'd be pushing away soon, and Blanche stayed on her balcony and drank in the winter warmth of California. It was so different from where she lived in New Jersey, which had been dealing with snow for a couple of weeks now.

She'd been dealing with cold, wintery storms in her heart since her husband's death, nine months ago. Tears didn't immediately come to her eyes the way they had so often in the past, but the deep ache in her heart, in her very soul, had her retreating from the railing and sinking into one of the deck chairs beside the small table-for-two.

Blanche had taken many a cruise in her lifetime. Once, she'd traveled on a cruise ship—one fifty times as big as this yacht—and done her stand-up routine every night the ship wasn't getting reserviced.

For over a year, she'd done that. She'd met Gregory on the cruise ship, and she'd quit the job to continue their relationship on solid ground. They'd been married a year later, and Blanche had exploded onto the cable network comedy scene a couple of years following that. They'd been together for forty-one years, and a day had not passed in that time where she didn't speak to him.

His voice had been silent for the past eight months, three weeks, and four days, however, and Blanche had almost lost the sound of it. She'd kept his cellphone, and whenever she got desperate, she'd call it.

Not even Mitch knew she did that, and she hadn't brought her husband's phone on the cruise. Her girls hovered more now that their father was gone, but Blanche had managed to keep the phone calls a secret from her daughters too.

Everyone dealt with grief in their own way, and Blanche returned to the room and gathered the new journal she'd brought specifically for this journey. She'd been writing in a diary or a journal since she could hold a sparkly pink pen. Back when she was seven years old, she started every entry with "Dear Diary."

Now, Blanche simply dated her entries and wrote out her experiences and feelings. Some of her best bits came from her daily writing, and she had notebooks and notebooks of writing, not all of it personal.

She also carried an assortment of small notebooks with her in every purse or bag she owned, just in case she got a great joke or heard a word that made her smile. She'd been known to be the mother of a few punchlines, and Blanche loved standing on a stage, entertaining people for an evening.

Back on the verandah, Blanche sighed as she sank into the deck chair. She flipped open the book, admiring the completely blank page. So much potential existed in a brand-new, never inked page.

The whole world opened to her whenever she lowered a pen to something so yawning, so ready to accept whatever she put on it, so beautiful. Yes, beautiful. Blanche found her hopes and dreams, love and friendship, acceptance and belonging, right there on the blank page.

Anything could happen. Anything at all.

She dated the top of the page, the blue ink flowing from her favorite pen and creating small scratching noises that got caught up with the lapping of the waves against the yacht.

It started to move, and Blanche looked up from her world of possibilities. A smile settled on her face, and she wasn't sure where it had come from. The sun shone strong over the ocean, making the water look like it was dancing with white light. The pair jumped and glittered, and yes, Blanche could admit her nerves were doing the same thing.

She was excited to be here, and she hadn't wanted to come at all. She'd fought Mitch every step of the way, but her older brother had a way of getting her to do exactly what he wanted. He always had.

With her eyes back on the blue ink, she started to write.

Well, I'm aboard the Sweet Sea Dreams. *The bed looks*

lovely, like a fresh vat of white cotton candy that, if I sink into it, I might never get out.

The water is a bit gray here, this close to the California coast, but the weather is supposed to be "glorious" for the next couple of weeks, and the receptionist who checked us in promised we'd have miles and miles of blue blue blue water.

Blanche relaxed further as her fingers formed the letters in her tale. Writing soothed her, as did the motion from the boat, and she felt herself drift.

Her phone buzzed, and she opened her eyes, not realizing she'd closed them. Her phone had a notification at the top she didn't recognize, so she swiped it open to check it.

The door to your suite has been opened, the message read, and it had a tiny black boat in a circle.

She twisted just as the sliding glass door opened and Mitch stepped onto her balcony. "Yours looks like mine," he said.

"They're the same type of room," she said. "Of course it looks like yours."

"I like this side better." He went to the railing and looked out over the water. "My side just shows the city."

For now, Blanche wanted to tell him.

The yacht moved at a steady clip now, turning away from the continent completely. Blanche experienced a sudden blip of panic, of leaving solid ground behind completely. Then her sea legs reminded her that she'd be okay out here, even if she hadn't wanted to come.

"Did you find your life jacket?" Mitch turned and gave her a mischievous grin. "Go through the safety card?" He came toward her and took the second chair on the opposite side of the tiny table. He glanced at her journal. "Ah, you're writing."

He beamed at her, and Blanche gave him a smile in return. It wasn't as clownish or as bright as his, but she'd always been dull compared to Mitch.

"What about running into Jenn?" she asked. "That's crazy, isn't it?"

"Serendipitous," he murmured, his eyes still past the railing and out there in the huge expanse of sky and water.

"You think so?" Blanche closed her notebook. She didn't have much to say, though she loved describing the places she stayed and visiting. "You think it's *serendipitous* that she's on the same cruise as us?"

Mitch looked at her then, more distance accumulating between them and solid land. The air smelled fresh and clean, and Blanche waited for her brother to speak. The breeze tugged at her short curls, and she reached up to tame them.

That had never really worked, and her hand dropped back to the now-closed notebook.

"Yes," he said. "There's one hundred people on this ship, Blanche. I think it's serendipitous your best friend from college is one of them."

"I'm okay," she said, tucking her pen into the coil of the notebook. "I don't need a 'special friend' to go around with me for the next two weeks." She gave her brother a look she hoped would cow him.

Mitch simply looked back at her.

Blanche didn't want to have this conversation. Unless someone had lost a spouse the way she had, no one could truly understand her. No one understood the dozens, then hundreds, then thousands of what-if's she'd played through her mind during her sleepless nights. During the day. While she burned her breakfast.

No one understood. Not even Mitch.

"Come on." She stood. "We said we'd meet her for lunch."

Mitch watched her, and Blanche hated that more than anything. "You need to meet a woman," she said, pointing a finger at him. "Then you'll leave me alone."

Her brother got to his feet, his smile finally reappearing. "Who says I haven't already met a woman?" His blue eyes flittered and glinted and danced the way the sunlight did off the water.

"Who?" Blanche demanded, but Mitch just rounded the table and her and re-entered her suite. He did not pull the sliding door closed behind him, leaving Blanche to scramble after him.

"Who?" she asked again.

But all he said was, "We don't want to be late to lunch with Jenn."

Chapter Four

Jennifer hung her slacks in the full-size closet and turned back to her suitcase. Her bag of toiletries got stashed under the sink in the bathroom, and she zipped the luggage closed and rolled it into the closet too.

Because her room was one of the largest on the yacht, she had room to do that. In fact, a person could lie down and sleep in this dedicated closet, but Jennifer returned to the main living quarters.

Her room sported a full bathroom, minus the tub, a working desk with a television mounted to the wall above it, and an oversized, cushy chair in the corner beside the door to the closet. The king bed took up the middle of the room, and her outdoor living space made up half of the square footage of the room.

With her unpacking done, and this room her new home base for the next fifteen days, Jennifer finally allowed herself to go out onto the balcony through one of two exits—the one along the back wall. Her bed faced this wall of windows, and she couldn't wait to wake up with the golden glow of the sun coming through the sheer curtains.

Outside, she immediately took a deep breath, the air whipping for a moment and trying to steal away her hair. She tipped her head back, closed her eyes, and let the elements have their way with her. She struggled to find a word to describe how she felt, standing just outside her room, the rushing sound of water as the yacht sliced through it, the scent of salt and brine, the cool air in her nose and the warm sun on her skin.

"Free," she whispered as her eyes came open again. She felt free, and there was no better feeling in the whole world. She tugged her shawl around her shoulders, glad she'd packed it though she'd felt a little foolish as she had. At the very least, she'd need it as the yacht cut through the waves as they returned to New York City.

That situation felt light years away, as the cruise was just beginning, and Jennifer had so many days and experiences to get through before she'd be on the East Coast again.

She turned her attention to her balcony, which held two loungers pointed toward the back of the ship. Her suite was officially labeled the "yacht suite," and there were only two rooms like this on the whole ship.

A sectional couch sat against the outdoor wall, with a table and two cushioned seats in front of it. Around the corner, she had an outdoor breakfast nook, with a small table and two chairs waiting just outside the sliding glass doors on the side of her room.

Sweet Sea Dreams did not disappoint, that was for sure. She snapped a few pictures and did a quick video of the outdoor amenities, the worries and burdens she carried growing lighter with each moment she spent out here.

She sent the video to her granddaughters back in Five Island Cove, and added, *You guys would love this balcony. We should take a cruise together next Christmas.*

Mandie had gone to college in New York City this year, but she always answered Jennifer's texts. It might take her a day or so, because she worked a lot and attended her classes on top of that.

Jamie still lived at home with Robin and Duke, and she was of the age where her phone never left her sight for longer than four seconds. She answered first, saying, *Wow, Grandma! Look at that place. A cruise would be amazing.*

Good luck convincing Mom, Mandie said, immediately sending a smiley face afterward.

Jennifer smiled too, because Mandie was absolutely right. *Maybe if we start working on her now, she'll warm up to the idea.*

Dad fishes too much in the winter, Mandie said. *I don't think he'd think a vacation should be spent on a boat.*

True, Duke lived his whole life on a boat, going out every day to fish the waters of the Atlantic.

Either way, Jennifer told her granddaughters. *I wish you two were here with me.*

She wasn't sure how long she'd spent in her suite, but another text popped up, this one from Blanche. *Mitch and I are on our way to the Crown Grill, on the Panorama Deck. I think it's the third one. Not sure where your room is or if you still want to join us.*

Jennifer didn't want to spend five figures on a cruise to sit in her room, even if it was big, with a gorgeous view of seemingly the entire world just off the balcony.

Her fingers flew as she typed out a response. *I'm on the Coastal Deck. I think that's one below Panorama, so I won't be long.*

Great, Blanche responded, and Jennifer returned to her room and checked her appearance in the mirror. She smoothed down her hair from where the wind had tried to take it off her head, and turned to look at the three wigs she'd brought with her.

Her own honeyed hair had been thinning for years, and she'd recently been introduced to the world of wigs. She owned about eight, but she'd only brought her three favorites with her on this trip.

Since she didn't want to shock Blanche and Mitch, who had seen her in her regular hair, she decided to go with a shorter style than she naturally wore in a color only two shades darker than hers.

She quickly smoothed her hair up onto her head and covered it with a wig cap. The shorter style went on easily, and Jennifer tugged the wig into the right place and arranged the hair so it lay the way she wanted it to. The hair had a wave in it, and the tips nearly brushed her shoulders.

This fashionable style took ten years off her shoulders, and she reached into her purse to reapply her lipstick. Her mother had taught her that no matter the chaos raging inside her life, her heart, or her mind, she could always give the appearance of being perfectly put together with a few quick swipes of lipstick.

With Jennifer's lighter hair and complexion—especially this deep into the winter—she chose a deep ruby red lipstick. It wasn't the bright red of Taylor Swift, or a light pink of a teenager. No. Jennifer wore a rich color of red that wasn't quite all the way to brick red. It enhanced her somewhat thin lips and made her feel like a million bucks, so her mother had been right.

Jennifer paused again to look at herself, pleased with the transformation a new hairstyle and a tube of lipstick could provide.

She didn't look like the same person who had gotten on the ship an hour ago, and she could only imagine how Blanche and Mitch would react to the change. The very idea brought a smile to her face.

Jennifer loved "hiding" behind her wigs, because it felt like a secret only she knew.

She hadn't changed out of her sensible slacks and white blouse with a black zigzag pattern on it, but it was the first day. She wouldn't be expected to be in her bathing suit, a fashionably bright cover-up, and her wide-brimmed beach hat until tomorrow.

She didn't need money here, so she slipped her purse and her tote bag with her laptop into the safe, set the code, and left her cabin.

With her room positioned at the back of the ship, she had to walk down the hall toward the middle of it, where the elevator was located. Two men waited there, and both of them smiled at her.

Nothing fizzed inside her this time, but she said, "Hello, gentlemen," anyway.

"Hello," they both said in return, and the elevator car arrived with a *ding*! They allowed her to get on first, and she nodded to both of them as she did.

The Panorama Deck was indeed one above hers, so the ride lasted only a few seconds. All three of them got off, and one of the men, who couldn't really have been over sixty, turned to her. "Do you have lunch plans? You could eat with us." He looked over to the other gentleman.

Jennifer put her best smile on her face. "I do. I'm meeting some friends. I'm so sorry."

The man grinned and waved away her apology. "No problem. I just didn't want you to be alone." His eyes zipped down to her feet and back to her face. "I'm Jeremy. Maybe we could get together for another meal."

He put out his hand, and Jennifer, as surprised as she was, did what any normal human being would do: She shook his hand and said, "Jennifer."

"Jeremy and Jennifer," his friend said. "That's cute." He smiled too, but Jennifer felt too old for "cute."

"Jennifer," a deep voice said, the sound of it almost humming through her bloodstream.

She turned toward the sound, her heartbeat quivering, and met Mitchell's eyes. "Oh," she said, because that popping and fizzing had started again. This time in her stomach, where it moved swiftly up into her lungs.

He put his hand on the small of her back and said, "We got a table by the windows, and the view is fabulous."

"Great." Jennifer turned back to the two men. "Great to meet you two." She nodded politely at them and turned with Mitchell. She noted that he wore a hard, almost dangerous look in his eye, and it wasn't until they'd arrived at the table that she realized what it was.

Warning.

He'd literally just claimed her as his, and as Jennifer spread a napkin in her lap, she wasn't sure how she felt about that. A quick glance over to Mitchell confirmed that the look had fled. Still. She'd seen it.

He smiled warmly now and said, "We've been here for five minutes." His eyes traveled across her face and hair. "I love your new hairdo."

"Thank you." Jennifer deliberately didn't reach up and touch her hair. Instead, she turned to Blanche, who also wore her hair short. "We're almost twins."

"Yes." Blanche lifted a glass of water to her lips and drank. "Oh." She hurriedly plunked the glass down as her eyes widened. "I was just telling Mitch here about the dastardly frat boy who made me wet my pants. Remember that?" Her eyes sparkled like starshine. "He didn't believe me."

Blanche Gibb was one of those people who was so beautiful she made everyone feel like they'd win a prize if they looked at her long enough. Besides her gold-blonde advantage, she was petite and curvy, and she wore her enthusiasm for the world to see.

"Only you," Mitch said with a laugh. "Only *you* could be talking about a dripping vehicle and make it funny." He reached across the table, grabbed a menu and a wine list, and handed both to Jennifer. She gave him an inquiring look, and he nodded toward the wine list. "Do you drink?"

"Sometimes. But I think boarding a yacht requires wine." She gave him a smile she hoped communicated more than what she'd said verbally. "What are you having?"

"I don't know." He studied the wine list, leaving the conversation open for Blanche and Jennifer.

She glanced over to her friend. "I remember the frat boy, because you started dating him." She grinned at Blanche. "Dragged me to every party, saying we *had* to go, because you got your best material from drunk co-eds."

"And I did," Blanche said. "I rode those jokes for *decades*." She laughed, and the sound lit up the already bright gallery where the restaurant sat.

It was starting to get busier, and Jennifer was glad she hadn't dawdled for longer than she had. "You're not doing your set anymore."

Blanche shook her head, her eyes still bright, but her smile sliding a bit. "Nope. I retired from it. Sold some rights. All that jazz." She took another drink of water. "Now I'm just working through retirement with Mitch." She looked across the table to her brother, and Jennifer followed her gaze.

"You go by Mitch then?" she asked.

"Or Mitchell," he said.

"No, it's Mitch," Blanche said. "Do you still go by Jenn? Or did you go back to your formal full name?"

"It's not that formal," Jennifer said.

Blanche laughed, the timbre of it different that her previous light-hearted giggles. "It sure is, Jennifer."

Jennifer didn't want to defend her name, and thankfully, a waiter arrived at the table. "Can I get you three something besides water to drink?"

"Yes." Mitch cleared his throat. "I'm thinking of bottle of Sauvignon Blanc for the table." He raised his eyebrows at Blanche and then Jennifer.

She nodded, and added, "I'd love a ginger ale too, please."

"Anything else?"

"I want something with a little umbrella in it," Blanche said. "Frozen. Slushie. With alcohol. What have you got like that?"

"Blanche," Mitch said, that warning in his voice now.

"What?" she fired back. "You ordered a whole bottle of wine for two people." She looked at the waiter and then Mitch. "It's a cruise. I'm allowed to have a drink or two."

Mitch said nothing, and the waiter walked Blanche through the cocktails until she found one she wanted. When just the three of them remained at the table, Jennifer decided to break right through the icy tension with a question she was sure they'd all answer a hundred times as they continued to meet people on this yacht.

"So," she said. "What brings you two on this cruise together?"

Chapter Five

Blanche took a deep breath and looked around the airy restaurant. There weren't many tables here, but the yacht only held one hundred people. Probably half of them could eat in here at the same time.

She didn't want to tell Jenn—oops, Jennifer—about Gregory's death. Her face would change, collapsing in on itself as she realized what she'd forced Blanche to do.

Then the pity would come. The sorrow. The whispered words of apology, as if "I'm sorry" could bring someone back from the dead—or even make the pain of losing them okay. It couldn't, and as Blanche met Jennifer's eyes, she realized something.

This woman had lost her husband to death too, and far earlier than Blanche had.

After taking another sip of her lukewarm water, she set it down and cleared her throat.

"Well," she said. "The reason Mitch and I are here on

this cruise is because my Greg passed away recently." She paused, looking at Jennifer with soft eyes. "It's been...difficult for me. I—"

"She hasn't left the house in too long," Mitch interrupted, and Blanche threw him a hard look.

"I leave the house," she said.

"Taking your miniature poodle for a walk doesn't count." He grinned at her, no malice or sarcasm in sight. Of course her brother loved her. Blanche knew that. Everyone meant well, but what they didn't understand was that they didn't understand what she really needed.

"He thinks this cruise will be good for me. A breath of fresh air." She looked out the windows that ran from floor to ceiling here. A few tables dotted the balcony beyond, but they didn't mar the view of the ocean she had. "Find some peace, maybe."

"Maybe meet someone new," Mitch said.

"No." Blanche nearly barked the word, her eyes darting back to her brother. Yes, this was a singles cruise. No, Blanche wasn't looking for a new boyfriend.

Mitch nodded silently, his smile gone now, his expression unreadable. At least he wasn't arguing. He'd wanted to get away from the city too. From the hustle and bustle he was no longer a part of. Blanche knew what it meant to sever oneself from the life they'd always lived. Retirement could be hard on a person, even when they were ready for it.

Jennifer reached out to place a hand on Blanche's arm. "I'm sorry for your loss." She glanced at Mitch before adding, "And you? Do you need a breath of fresh air too?" She smiled, and Blanche liked that she could hold her own at the table, especially with Mitch. "Or did you come to meet someone new?"

Blanche grinned at her brother and raised her eyebrows. He rolled his eyes, but his smile quickly followed. "Maybe both," he admitted.

"Mm." Jennifer ducked her head, and Blanche finally put two and two together. The way Mitch continued to watch Jennifer. The way she played with her silverware, as if they needed rearranging.

"Sauvignon Blanc," the waiter said, appearing with the bottle and two wine glasses. "Ginger ale. And the Caribbean Surprise." Another man had come with him to deliver all the drinks, and the moment between Jennifer and Mitch broke—if it was even there.

Blanche definitely thought it was, but she'd wait for Mitch to bring it up. He'd given her the same courtesy after Greg's death, and Blanche appreciated that he had gotten her out of the house for this cruise.

She could only pray that her daughters wouldn't empty it of the things Blanche still wanted before she could return to it.

The following day, Blanche couldn't help but be proud of herself as she chatted with the other passengers at her table. Even though she hadn't planned to meet anyone new, that didn't mean she couldn't practice making small talk with strangers.

The woman across from her, whose name was Catherine, had been telling a story about how she'd met her husband on a singles cruise, many years ago. She seemed so happy that Blanche couldn't help but smile along with her.

Of course, she was once again on a singles cruise, and another man at the table finally asked, "Did you lose him, then?" He glanced at the others at the table, one man named Ben and another named Frank.

"Yes," Catherine said. "Several years ago." Her smile popped onto her face, and then slid away just as quickly. Blanche realized then that everyone on this ship was single for a reason. Death or divorce or they'd never married. No matter what, it was a depressing thought to think about any of those.

Condolences went around the table, and Blanche murmured her own. She didn't want to tell her story at all, so she lifted her lemonade to her lips and remained silent.

"Which restaurant are y'all eating at tonight?" Ben asked, and he'd already revealed he was from Texas.

"I've got a reservation at Grenada," Catherine said, looking around the table. "I guess they just give you a time, and then you get seated with the people in your same slot?" Her eyes harbored worry, and it ate at Blanche's gut.

Mitch had texted that morning to say he'd gotten

them reservations at Caribbean Trattoria, but Blanche held her tongue. Her phone buzzed, and the conversation began to do the same as she focused her attention on her device.

Mitch: *Is it okay if Jennifer comes to dinner with us tonight?*

Blanche read the text twice, her heartbeat fluttering in her chest. She worked to tamp down the panic. Of course Mitch wasn't going to ditch her for the next two weeks so he could pursue a romance with her old college roommate.

The very idea was the plot of a holiday movie, the kind that Blanche had been watching religiously for the past six decades of her life.

In that moment, she felt like her life had been one big lead-up to the things happening now. She *was* living in this Christmas romance movie of her brother's.

The retired prosecutor. A happy-go-lucky guy who's still really good looking, can make anyone laugh, and so lonely it hurts everyone watching. They immediately love him and want him and Jennifer to sail away—literally—toward their happily-ever-after.

The old college roommate. If there was a more obvious trope, Blanche had probably seen it a thousand times in the movies she'd consumed.

What role did she have? The loner? The "extra" that was required to interrupt first kisses and have long conversations with old friends and siblings alike?

Was she here for her own romance? She looked up at

Ben, Catherine, and Frank. She felt nothing for them; she could talk to them. Even be interested in what they said. But there was nothing romantic between her and either of the men at this table.

She honestly didn't think she'd ever feel like that about someone again.

Mitch: *You're not answering. Did you go back to your room to write?*

She scoffed under her breath, though the quiet and solace of her room did call to her.

Before she could answer, another text came in from her brother. *Did you fall asleep while reading? I'm coming to your room right now.*

I'm not in my room, she quickly typed out. *You're interrupting my lunch.*

She still didn't answer his question, and Mitch would hate that. He'd follow-up too, but Blanche decided to make him. She'd had to answer a lot of his hard questions in the past several months, and the longing for easier times slipped through her.

A single slice of toast remained on the bruschetta platter, and Blanche picked it up and popped it into her mouth as all eyes came to her.

She chewed quickly and said, "My brother and I are dining at the Italian restaurant tonight."

"What time?" Frank asked, his eyes glinting as he smiled.

"You know, I'm not sure," Blanche said. "He handled it all."

They peered at her. Or maybe they were just looking at her. Blanche felt under the microscope all the time, and she'd told everyone around her there was no reason to inspect her life so closely.

Because if they did... Well, Blanche had a few skeletons in her closet. Who didn't?

Eden will skewer you when she finds out about the late-night shopping.

The thought sprang into her mind, and no matter how hard she pushed, it would not leave. The conversation at the table moved on, but Blanche's mind focused on her spending habits and bills since Gregory's death.

She'd handle them. No one else needed to know, not her daughter, not Mitch, and certainly not these three near-strangers. Eating one meal with a person did not make them a friend.

For that matter, running into an old college roommate after forty years didn't make her and Jennifer friends either. At the same time, Blanche ached to tell someone of the things she'd bought on the Shopping Station, and she suspected Jennifer would understand better than anyone.

Mitch had lost his wife to a divorce. They still spoke to each other, of course. In fact, he was better friends with her now than he had been when they'd been married. He didn't understand the grieving process after the death of a spouse, and Blanche wasn't spending money she didn't have.

Yet.

She turned over her phone when it started buzzing and wouldn't stop. Mitch's name sat on the screen, and she swiped on the call as she backed up from the table. "She can come. My goodness, you're relentless."

"You don't look like you're having fun."

She stood and scanned the outdoor area for Mitch. She'd gone to lunch on the Pool Deck, where an outdoor cafe served light appetizers and lunch fare.

Her brother stood near the end of the bar, and Blanche lowered her phone. "It was lovely to meet you," she gushed at her lunch partners. "Thank you for entertaining me during lunch." She nodded toward the bar. "I have to meet my brother."

"I hope we'll see you again," Frank said, and she wondered if he spoke for everyone or if he meant *he* hoped *he'd* see her again.

Her pulse skittered through her veins like a terrified rabbit at the thought of the latter, and she nodded quickly before making her escape.

This cruise.

As Jennifer stepped to Mitch's side, her smile wide and beautiful as she drank in the Pool Deck before her, Blanche thought, *Maybe it wasn't such a great idea after all.*

Chapter Six

Jennifer rolled over in bed and looked at the clock embedded into the wall there. She'd never been able to sleep very late, a condition that had only worsened as she'd aged.

This morning, thoughts of Robin plagued her. The yacht should be pulling into the dock in Puerto Vallarta within minutes, and Jennifer wondered how many people aboard-ship had their gear ready for a day on dry land.

She'd signed up for a half-day of horseback riding, and her alarm would go off in another five minutes so she could get up and shower. She'd packed her backpack and her beach bag last night, because after the morning ride through the "picturesque countryside" of the Jalisco region of Mexico, she'd have a few hours to spend on the beach.

With her alarm silenced, Jennifer stepped into the

shower a few minutes early. She exited her suite twenty minutes later, not expecting to see Mitch standing outside her room but not entirely surprised either.

"No Blanche?" she asked, her heart swooping and diving behind her ribs. At the same time, it sank toward the soles of her feet, only getting yanked back into place by the veins and arteries holding it where it needed to be.

Mitch shook his head, his bright blue eyes sparkling. "She said she hasn't ridden a horse a day in her life, and she's not going to start now." He extended his hand toward Jennifer, and she easily gave him her beach bag and then slipped her hand into his other one. A thrill moved through her. "She'll meet us on the beach later."

"So at least she'll get off the ship," Jennifer said.

"Mm."

They started toward the walkway that would lead them off the yacht. Jennifer didn't know what to say all of sudden. She'd spent the past couple of days at sea with Mitch and Blanche, catching up and enjoying delicious meals, inventive shows, and ruminating on what she could say to her daughter to make things right.

"Can I ask you a question?" she asked.

"Of course," he said. "Though, just because I'm a lawyer—was a lawyer—doesn't mean I can give you legal advice." He grinned at her, and Jennifer returned the gesture.

"This isn't legal advice," she said. She had a perfectly good lawyer in Five Island Cove who reviewed any contract or document before Jennifer signed it. Besides,

Mitch had practiced criminal law, a completely different branch of the law than what Jennifer would ever need.

"It's about my daughter."

"Robin," he said, as they'd spoken of their children in the time they'd spent together. Mitch had three adult children; two sons and a daughter, and Robin knew their names too.

"Yes," she said. "We don't...see eye-to-eye on some things." She drew in a breath as they encountered the line and had to slow their step. "Fine. All things. We barely talk. When we do, it's superficial things about the weather and her work."

"Not yours?"

"There's nothing that happens at a small dentist's office in a small island community." Jennifer flashed him a smile that disappeared in the next moment. "I wish...I wish I knew how to talk to her. How to fix the things I've done wrong."

Mitch nodded, but he didn't launch into the advice-giving. The line moved forward again, and within a minute, they'd left *Sweet Sea Dreams* behind and set foot in Mexico. He took a big breath and held it for a moment. "I didn't hear a question in any of that."

Jennifer shook her head, because she hadn't asked one. She didn't know the right one to ask. "You said one of your sons...strayed and then came back. How did you handle that?"

Again, Mitch didn't answer for a moment. His grip on her hand tightened as he redirected the pair of them toward the excursion waiting area for the horseback riding. The participant limit had been capped at twelve, and it looked like it would be full this morning.

The cruise line didn't allow for any advance registrations for excursions at the ports. It was a singles cruise, after all, and Mitch had been able to secure these two spots for them with the app on his phone. Jennifer hated getting notifications from every app under the sun, so she'd turned hers off.

Mitch hadn't, and he'd reserved two tickets for the horseback riding—the limit a single cruiser could do—and Jennifer had then gotten on the app and scheduled her afternoon beach time. They had to be back on the yacht by five o'clock tonight, where they'd eat in the Stateroom, again at a table of six.

Three new people to meet, and Jennifer had actually felt bad for the trios they'd been sitting with at dinner the past couple of nights. It hardly seemed fair that they had to sit down alone, without knowing a soul, and Blanche, Mitch, and Jennifer all knew one another.

Last night, Jennifer could admit she'd ignored everyone except for Mitch. Not intentionally, but that didn't mean it hadn't happened.

Resolved to do better tonight, her conversation with Mitch got put on hold while a man wearing an oversized sombrero checked them in for their excursion. He introduced himself as Pablo, "a four-generation charro."

He wore a white shirt with elaborate embroidery in burnt red along the cuffs, up the front where the buttons sat, and along the chest and shoulders. A tie sat around his throat, and the only way Jennifer knew how to describe it was fluffy. It matched the red in the thread, as did his pants. He wore boots on his feet along with his hat, and he looked like a traditional Mexican gentlemen.

Jennifer's mood lightened—until she had to get on her steed. That was quite impossible, as she was exactly like Blanche—she hadn't ridden a horse in forty years. Perhaps longer.

Thankfully, Pablo provided assistance and stools for anyone who needed it, and by the time Jennifer sat in the saddle, her face burned with embarrassment but she hadn't been the only one struggling to get atop the horse.

Mitch looked over to her. "Ready?"

She nodded and reached up to smooth her hair. She'd left her wigs in the room this morning, because they weren't known for being cool, and she could cover her thinning hair with a hat. She did that, wondering where her beach bag had gone.

"My bag?" she asked Mitch.

"I checked it with the matron," he said. "You didn't see me?"

"I was getting on my horse." She held her head high as a Cheshire-Cat grin crossed Mitch's face. "Stop it."

"Stop what?" He expertly maneuvered his horse closer to hers and reached for her hand.

"I can't." She clung to the reins, hoping she wouldn't have to actually steer this animal. "This might've been a mistake." Her back and hips ached already from how hard she had to work to keep herself in the saddle. "How long will this be?"

Mitch chuckled, a deep, sexy sound that hummed through Jennifer's chest. "It's four hours, hon. Do you want to call an audible and slip away to the beach now?" He seemed like he'd give up his chance to ride through the beautiful countryside if she wanted to slide from the saddle now.

"No." She shook her head. "We took these slots from other people." She managed to position her hat on her head without falling off the horse. "I'm ready."

Mitch faced Pablo as he swung into his saddle. "They know we're in our sixties," he said. "We can have them stop any time."

Jennifer nodded, and Pablo turned his horse. The other equines fell into step, giving Jennifer a sense of relief that she wasn't really expected to do much except enjoy the ride. She relaxed slightly, and managed to focus on more than not falling.

"The hardest conversation is the first one," Mitch said after a couple of minutes.

Jennifer looked over to him, her eyebrows up.

"With your daughter." He cut her a look out of the corner of his eye. "Just get your favorite drink nearby, and promise yourself you won't drink it until the conversation is over."

"Like a reward?"

"Yes," he said. "Not a drop beforehand. You want to be calm and levelheaded. I can't say it'll be easy, but I know you love a good glass of red, and you like to sip it slowly in good company." He reached over and brushed his fingertips along her forearm. "So let me bring it to you tonight—after you talk to Robin."

"As a celebration," she murmured even as her anxiety started to thrum. She couldn't commit to it verbally, but she did nod, and with that settled, Mitch withdrew his hand. She listened as Pablo pointed out the beauty surrounding them, as Jennifer had never been to this part of Mexico before.

Every moment, every breath, brought a new experience, and she wanted to be present for all of them. She wanted to be able to reflect on them later, not wonder why she'd let her mind distract her from the things right in front of her now.

The first conversation is the hardest.

But Jennifer had done hard things in the past. She'd buried her husband far too early. She'd returned home, and after all the well-wishers had gone, she'd been alone. After all the casseroles had been eaten, she'd had to go through things alone. After her mother had left, and her children had gone back to their regular lives, Jennifer had had to figure out what "normal" meant for her.

She'd had to go through her husband's secrets. She'd had to shoulder them, and then manage them.

She could call her daughter and have a hard conversation.

LATER THAT EVENING, JENNIFER HAD SHOWERED the sunscreen from her skin. She'd enjoyed a beautiful day off the yacht, and she could still feel the sand between her toes. Having grown up on Long Island, and then living the majority of her adult life on Five Island Cove, she was no stranger to the beach. She craved it, and she loved the sound of the ocean greeting the shore, and the feel of fine grains of sand covering her feet.

She currently wore a pair of wide-leg white pants and a blue-and-white striped tank top. No shoes, as she wasn't planning on leaving her suite again. She stepped from the room to the balcony, the night air chilly against her bare arms.

She lived on an island, and she well knew the press of darkness that came from wide open water. There were no streetlamps or front porch lights to break up the endless, consuming darkness as it covered open water, but Jennifer found it oddly comforting.

Tonight, the moon shone onto the surface of the ocean from the opposite side of the yacht, almost creating a shadow beyond her railing. She wouldn't be able to stand out here for long, but she wanted to make the phone call to her daughter without a ceiling hanging over her head.

It was getting late in Five Island Cove now, and Jennifer quickly retreated to her room, grabbed a jacket and her phone, and faced the sliding glass doors she hadn't closed when she'd come inside.

"He'll be here in forty-five minutes," she murmured

to herself. She had to make this call, or she'd have to tell Mitch she hadn't done it. Then he'd have purchased that expensive bottle of wine for no reason.

She *wanted* to do this, and she reminded herself of that fact as she donned the jacket and started swiping on her phone. It was time to be brave, something that she marveled was still hard for a woman of her age and experiences. But it was.

It was time to do this hard thing. It was time to be vulnerable. It was time to perhaps apologize and admit that she wasn't always right.

Her tongue got caught against the roof of her mouth as she tried to swallow, and she coughed a couple of times trying to dislodge the fear that had suddenly formed a lump against her windpipe.

She found Robin's name at the top of the list of people she'd been texting, and she tapped to call her, hardly any air in her lungs for talking.

Chapter Seven

Robin Glover sat up in bed, her wedding planner laid over her lap, when her phone rang. Her mother's face sat there, and the fight left Robin's body.

Beside her, her husband stirred. Duke could sleep through almost anything, which was why Robin liked working in bed beside him, only her lamp throwing light around the room. She didn't want to wake him, however, so she swiped on the call and lifted the phone to her ear in almost the same motion. "Mom," she whispered. "Give me two seconds to get into the kitchen, okay?"

"Okay, dear," her mother said, her voice as refined as ever.

Robin slipped quickly from the king-size bed she shared with the love of her life, and she padded down the hall and around the corner to her kitchen. Her oldest lived in New York City now, unhurt though she'd been hit by a courier on a bicycle. That job in the winter was no joke, and the bike had been equipped with hand warmers and a crate for carrying deliveries.

Mandie had been checked out at the hospital, and she'd been deemed fine. A few scrapes and bruises that were mostly healed. The semester at NYU had ended that same day, and Robin had brought her daughter home to Five Island Cove for the holidays.

She had her own room on the second floor of this new house she and Duke had purchased recently, where her youngest slept too. Jamie was fourteen going on forty, and Robin sighed as she opened the fridge and took out a bottle of water she knew she wouldn't drink.

"I'm sorry if it's too late," her mother said. "I forget I'm on the West Coast."

"Puerto Vallarta looked amazing," Robin said instead of reassuring her mother it wasn't too late. The clock had just ticked past eleven p.m. here, so it was late.

"It was," her mother said. "I'd love to bring you and the family sometime. You would love cruising."

Robin wasn't sure how to answer. Her mother had never offered to take Robin or her family, let alone all of them, on any type of vacation. Ever. "I've been on a lot of boats in my life," she said.

"A cruise is different."

Of course it was. Robin bit back the poisoned words and pressed her eyes closed. "I'm sure it is," she said evenly.

Silence poured through the line, and Robin opened

her eyes again. Something was different about her mother. "Mom?"

Her mom cleared her throat. "Robin, I would like to apologize to you."

Robin's mouth fished open and closed as she tried to find a response.

"I owe you a great many explanations about...things." Another grind through her mother's throat told Robin how difficult this conversation was for her. "My finances, for one. The decisions I've made with them, for another. I'd really like it if, when I return to the cove, we can sit down, and I can show you some things."

Robin moved over to her dining room table and collapsed into one of the chairs. "Yeah," she said. "I'd like that too."

"Your father had accumulated a great deal of wealth," her mother continued. "I've been doing my best to manage it, and well, I fear I've gone a little bit too far."

Robin's heartbeat skipped. "Too far?"

"I've been too conservative." Her mother let another bout of silence invade the line, but this time, Robin didn't prompt her. "I have regretted every single day since the tsunami that I didn't simply purchase you and Duke a new fishing boat."

Again, Robin found herself without words. She didn't want to tell her mother it was okay, because when Duke's boat had been shattered in the tsunami, that had been a horribly devastating time in Robin's life. So much so that she'd almost borrowed money from someone she shouldn't have to get him back on his feet. Get *them* back on their feet.

His fishing supported their family, and Robin had taken on more and more clients to make ends meet and pay for a brand-new boat so Duke could continue to run his business too.

"If you'll allow me to," her mom continued, her voice far more choked now. It pitched up and down, crackled and yawned, the way a boat did over rolling waves. "I'd appreciate the opportunity to pay for it now. Clear it from your expenses completely."

"Mom." The air whooshed out of Robin's lungs with the word. Her brain couldn't find a thought to latch onto. "You—" She wasn't sure how to continue. She didn't want to tell her mother she didn't have to do that. They both knew that already.

"It wouldn't even put a dent in the money I have," her mom whispered. "Please, Robin. I am so sorry." Her voice broke on the last word, and Robin found her own eyes burning with tears.

Questions marched through her mind, but this deep into the night was no time to fire them at her mother. "Let's sit down together when you return," she said, her own voice catching against the soft tissue in her throat. "Okay?"

"I would so love that," her mom said. "Do you think...?" She let the question hang there, and Robin knew now that her pregnant pauses came from her emotions. Her mother hated showing emotion, and in fact, she rarely had. The one Robin was most acquainted with was anger, as she and her mother had argued and fought a great deal over the years. They were too much alike, and Robin thought of the numbers she'd been writing in her planner before this call had come in.

She was meticulous with a budget too, a trait she'd inherited from the woman on the phone. She had no idea what situation her mother had been put in when her father had died, but Robin couldn't help but wonder if she'd have done the same thing as her mom.

Taken things too far. Been too conservative. Too afraid to spend even a dime of the money her deceased husband had left her.

"Do you think you could meet me in New York?" her mom finally asked. "You and the family. I return on the thirtieth. Might you be returning Mandie to the city about then?"

"We might be," Robin said. "I can check my calendar when I go back to bed."

"Oh, you were in bed? Why did you answer?"

"I was working," Robin quickly assured her, though she felt chastised by her mom's questions. She could answer if she was asleep or not. She was grown woman.

"Could you perhaps ask Stu if he might come?"

Robin's lungs once again emptied of air. "Mom, I don't know about that."

"I need to call him and apologize too." She sighed, but it wasn't one of her self-important ones. "It's so hard to apologize for so many years, so many conversations, so many missed opportunities, in one sentence."

Yes, it was. One blanket apology didn't make up for everything over the years, but at the same time, it did. With the help of her husband and daughters, a lot of running on the beach in the mornings, and her work, Robin had been able to let go of some of the things her mother had done that had injured her.

"I'll talk to him if you will," Robin said. "Mom, just start the call the same way you did with me."

"He won't take my calls."

Robin looked out the sliding glass door to the darkness beyond. She and Duke had hosted several barbecues and get-togethers in this backyard since they'd moved in. She loved her friends here in Five Island Cove, as well as her clients. She'd grown up here, fallen in love here, and raised her family here.

She loved the cove with her whole heart, and she couldn't wait to dissect this phone call with Alice, Eloise, and Laurel tomorrow. The four of them were set to have lunch to plan a surprise birthday party for Kristen, their Seafaring Girls teacher from decades ago.

"I don't know what to tell you," Robin finally said when the darkness wouldn't give her any answers. "Relationships are two-way streets, Mom. At some point, he decided it wasn't worth the drive."

"I know." Another sigh, this one heavy and full of tears. "I'll try anyway, and maybe you can advocate for me. Perhaps simply tell him to pick up the phone? I'll do all the talking."

"I'll try," Robin said, though she knew deep in her soul that the reason her mom found herself in the predicament she did with both Robin and Stu was because of her mouth.

The words she said had cut deep, deep wounds, and they couldn't be taken back. Robin had been learning to hold her tongue more and more as her girls grew up, because the one thing she never, ever wanted to be was her mother.

She wanted open, honest relationships with her girls, yes. She would not use her words as weapons the way her mom had.

"I love you, dear." Her mother's wounded voice brought a fresh round of tears to Robin's eyes. "I love you so much." She was definitely crying, and she didn't seem to be holding back now. She wasn't trying to compose herself before she spoke. "Please tell the girls and Duke that I love them too, and please accept my apologies. To you. To them. For anything I've done."

"Mom," Robin said. "Of course we will."

Sniffling came through the line, and then, as Jennifer Golden often did, she drew a drawstring and bundled everything back together. "Thank you, dear. I'm sorry to wake you."

"I was working," Robin said again, opening the door for her mom to jab at her for working so late at night, something she'd done before.

Tonight, though, her mother simply said, “We’ll talk soon.”

“I love you, Mom.” Robin’s chest stormed with emotion, because she did love her mother. There were some bonds that were terribly hard to break, and though things had been said and feelings hurt for a great many years, that didn’t mean they couldn’t be healed.

“Robin, I love you with everything I have.”

Tears slid down Robin’s face, and she nodded. All she’d ever wanted was to be loved and accepted by her mother. Over the years, she’d worked tirelessly to make her proud, and nothing had ever been good enough.

Until that simple sentence. Robin heard the depth of emotion in it, and she knew—she *knew*—that her mother loved her. Her mother was proud of her, of how she’d raised her family, of how she’d been living her life.

“We’ll talk tomorrow,” her mom whispered, and then the call ended. Robin let her hand fall to her lap as the screen on her phone went dark. She wept in near silence as she imagined her mother thousands of miles away, obviously hurting and thinking about the things she needed to apologize for.

“Baby?”

She looked over to her husband’s tall form, front lit by the soft glow from the light above the stove.

“My mom called.” Her voice came out nasally, and Duke hurried toward her.

He dropped into a crouch in front of her, his hands

protectively sweeping her device away as he asked, "What did she say? Why did you answer?"

Of course he'd assume her mother had said something hurtful or cruel. She had so often in the past; why would this call, even as close to Christmas as it was, be any different?

Robin shook her head and wiped her face. "She apologized, Duke."

"What?"

"She said she wants to pay for the boat."

In the low light, Duke searched her face. A smile began to tug at the corners of Robin's mouth. "She *apologized*."

"Are you sure it was her?"

Robin laughed lightly, the sound only landing for a moment. "It was her. It was like she was...broken." Her smile and joy receded. "She's broken, Duke. And she's going to need all of us to help put her back together."

She reached out and cupped her husband's face in her hand. "Will you help me put her back together?"

He rose to his feet and took her hand. "Come back to bed," he whispered. "You can tell me everything she said, and we'll figure out what to do."

Chapter Eight

Blanche watched as water churned behind the yacht. It wasn't as big as the ships that carried thousands, but the vessel still stirred up plenty of water, turning it white and leaving a footprint behind them.

"You dropped out early."

She looked over to Jennifer, who looked like a celebrity in her oversized sunglasses, a snow-white cover up, with just the hint of her bright pink swimming suit showing at the throat, and a glass of something alcoholic in her hand. Her hair today fell halfway down her back in dark waves, and Blanche had been seriously considering buying some wigs once she returned to Jersey.

No one could pull things off the way Jennifer could, though. Blanche would likely end up looking like a clown instead of a fabulously aged supermodel.

"I hate trivia," Blanche said, turning her attention

back to the water. "I never should've let you talk me into it."

Jennifer laughed and bumped Blanche with her hip. "You've liked some of the things I've talked you into."

"Name one."

"The coffee tour and hanging bridges we literally did yesterday."

Blanche couldn't argue with that one. She had enjoyed the walk through the lush Costa Rica rain forests, with those gorgeous hanging bridges that seemed to be suspended from heaven itself. "Fine," she muttered. "I'm surprised *you* enjoyed it though."

"Why wouldn't I enjoy it?"

Blanche didn't want to be petty. Mitch had been plenty attentive to her so far. As today was day seven of the cruise, and they'd be going through the Panama Canal the day after tomorrow, Blanche could admit she'd enjoyed her vacation so far.

She'd met some fabulous people here on the yacht. She'd seen couples starting to pair off, of course. She'd had some of the best meals of her life. She couldn't expect Mitch to stick by her side twenty-four-seven.

And yet, she hadn't expected him to fall for her old college roommate either. She hadn't expected to be a third wheel, though she'd known this was a singles cruise.

"Mitch wasn't there," she said bluntly.

Jennifer may have blinked behind her shades; Blanche would never know. She didn't miss a beat as she said, "I had a fantastic time without him. Didn't you?"

Blanche had, so she said as much. Jennifer twisted and set her drink down. She linked her arm through Blanche's. "I could introduce you to a man or two," she said under her breath. "I've seen several of them eyeing you."

"If you do, I will never talk to you again."

Jennifer laughed lightly. "We weren't talking before this."

Blanche looked over to her, a measure of fear rising through her. "You promised we could stay in touch."

"We will."

A sigh pulled through Blanche. "I...I need someone to talk to about Gregory," she admitted. "Mitch just watches me and then says I need to give myself time. My daughters look at me like I might need to be committed." The water churned, churned, churned, mirroring everything inside Blanche. "I don't have anyone else."

Jennifer gave herself a moment before she asked, "What do you miss the most about him? When I lost Connor, I missed the way he'd call every time he got home from work."

Blanche looked over to her, noting the small smile and faraway look on her friend's face. "It was like clockwork," she continued. "He'd walk in the door every evening at six, and call, 'I'm home, sweets.' A few seconds later, he'd arrive in the kitchen, loosening his tie, and smiling at me. He never had a briefcase. He never brought it past the small office off the garage. He never polluted our family time with business."

"That's a good memory," Blanche said.

"After he died, I hated six o'clock," Jennifer said. "I couldn't even be home at that hour, and if I was, I'd been drinking for hours." She flashed a smile. "Robin almost had to intervene."

Blanche watched her for a moment, and then scoffed. "I don't believe that."

"Which part?"

"That Robin had to intervene." Blanche cocked one eyebrow at Jennifer. "You would've never allowed that."

Jennifer watched the water now. "Perhaps you're right, but I'd like to think my daughter was concerned about how much I was drinking after her father's death."

They stood side-by-side, the sound of the cocktail party behind them not quite covering the rushing sound of the water only a deck below.

"I shop," Blanche said, not sure why she'd said anything at all. She looked over to Jennifer, pure vulnerability making every cell in her body quake. "I shop all night long when I can't sleep. I shop in the middle of the afternoon when I miss the way Gregory would bring me cinnamon chip bagels from the shop down the street, brew a pot of coffee, and sit with me on the screened porch while I scribbled in my notebooks."

Jennifer didn't launch into a lecture about saving money or soothing herself with needless items. She simply nodded. "What do you buy?"

"Anything," Blanche said, her mind moving as fast as the ship, as fast as the earth spun through space, too fast.

"And everything. It makes me feel like I'm in control, after such a long time of being at the mercy of this doctor or that one, this treatment or that one, at watching him lose his very life, and I couldn't do anything—not one single thing—about it."

Tears appeared and splashed down her face. Blanche snapped back to herself then, turning away from Jennifer and wiping her face quickly. Humiliation seeped into her, and she couldn't believe what she'd just revealed.

"I have the money," she mumbled.

"Grief shopping is a real thing," Jennifer said gently. "You don't need to be embarrassed about it."

"Please don't tell Mitch." Blanche squared her shoulders and faced Jennifer. "I haven't told anyone but you, and I'd like to keep it between us."

Jennifer smiled. "Have you forgotten that I'm the best secret-keeper in the apartment?"

Blanche's memories fired at her, and a smile slowly spread her lips too. "I had forgotten that."

"Don't worry, Blanche." Jennifer laid her head against Blanche's shoulder. "I won't say anything."

"Miss Gibb?"

They both turned at the question, and Blanche found a sharply dressed woman standing a pace or two away. She wore the dark maroon jacket and black pants of the staff members on the yacht, her medium brown hair secured in its customary knot at the back of her head. All of the women wore their hair that way, minimal makeup, and professional smiles.

This woman flashed one now. "I'm the activities director." She extended her hand. "Nahvi Samuelson. I heard you were—are—a professional stand-up comedienne."

"No," Blanche said at the same time Jennifer said, "She is."

Their eyes met, and Blanche searched her friend's face. They hadn't seen each other for forty years, but they'd once been able to have silent conversations with these types of non-verbal communications. Jennifer was as sharp as ever, and she cleared her throat and turned back to Nahvi.

"She's retired."

Nahvi nodded. "I apologize. We've had one of our most popular performers come down with an illness. He's quarantined in his room, and I'm looking to fill the spot."

Blanche's interest pricked, and she didn't want to say no so fast anymore. "Nightly entertainment?"

"Yes," Nahvi confirmed. "Just for five nights. Tonight is off the table, as we've canceled the show and replaced it with this cocktail hour. It's day eight of our cruise tomorrow, so a show then, and for the following four evenings, until we arrive in Miami. There's no show that night, as we bring aboard some local performers from the city there."

"Five shows," Jennifer said.

"Five nights," Blanche said.

Jennifer looked at her again. "Did you bring your

notebooks?" she asked, though she had to know the answer to that question. Blanche had brought them to the upper deck yesterday, hoping to find a sunny spot to write down her thoughts.

Blanche didn't confirm one way or the other. She looked back to Nahvi. "Can I think about it and let you know?"

"Of course, ma'am." She nodded, her neck dipping so far it was a near bow. "You can pick up any phone and dial our receptionist and ask for me. She'll find me."

Blanche nodded, and the younger woman smiled curtly before she turned and left her standing with Jennifer.

"When's the last time you did a show?" Jennifer picked up her drink and wandered toward the party. Blanche went with her, though she had no interest in mixing and mingling. She didn't drink much, as it left her headachy the following morning. She was grateful for that now, after hearing how Jennifer had dealt with her grief.

Everyone had to do it in their own way, and Blanche didn't fault her for escaping into a stupor of liquor by six o'clock. Blanche had spent five figures on things she didn't need, and if she didn't stop soon, she'd have to buy a bigger house to hold everything.

"Oh, over a year ago." Blanche took a big breath and blew it out. "Even then, it was for charity. I retired a while ago, Jenn. People like young comedians."

"Not on this yacht, they wouldn't," she said casually.

She exchanged her drink for a fresh flute of Pinot Grigio and added, "I wish they had some of that Pinot Noir from the other night."

"You mean the night you and Mitch disappeared into your suite until all hours of the morning."

Jennifer's gaze flew to hers. "That is *not* what happened."

"Sure," Blanche said slyly. "I know my brother's phone was pinging from your suite until at least midnight, at which point I fell asleep."

"You watch his pin on the yacht?"

"I called him three times, and he wouldn't answer," Blanche said, lifting her chin an inch or two. "I feared he may have fallen overboard."

"You did not." Jennifer smiled and then started to laugh. "You were spying on him."

"Did he stay the night?"

"Absolutely not," Jennifer said, her voice filled with scandal.

"What?" Blanche said. She too plucked a glass of white wine from the silver tray offered to her. "Look around, Jenn. Look at all these happy couples who've formed in the past week. Just like you and Mitch. You don't think they're utilizing the privacy of their suites before this cruise ends and we all have to go back to our regular lives?"

"I have no idea," Jennifer said as she too scanned the party in front of them. She sipped her wine, her jaw tight. "I think a fifteen-day cruise was maybe a mistake."

"Really? Why?"

"Maybe just one on a boat this size," Jennifer clarified. "I feel...boxed in. Don't you?"

"There will be more ports once we get through the Panama Canal," Blanche said. They'd only stopped twice, once in Mexico and once in Costa Rica, in the past week. "The bulk of the sailing was on this end of the cruise."

"We've a long way to go," Jennifer said quietly, and Blanche wasn't sure if she was talking about the cruise or her relationship with Mitch. It could've gone either way. In the next moment, she brightened. "I think you should do the show."

"Of course you do." Blanche almost didn't want to do it, simply because Jennifer wanted her to. "Mitch will want me to as well."

"Think about that for a moment," Jennifer said. "Why do we want you to do it?"

"Because," Blanche said. "You like torturing me." She took a sip of her wine, not entirely hating the taste but not really liking it either. She'd simply hold it so she'd fit in.

"Yes," Jennifer murmured. "There is that." She bloomed to life as Mitch pushed past a couple who'd started dancing in the restaurant space where this cocktail party had been set up. He grinned at the pair of them as he came closer.

He took Blanche into his arms and whispered, "You look like you could stab me," in her ear before stepping back. His eyes asked her a thousand questions, and then he switched his attention to Jennifer. He definitely liked her, but Blanche would be surprised if they'd spent the night together already.

Neither of them were really the type to rush into things, and Mitch's divorce was only a few years old. He hadn't really started dating again, and he'd told her a man his age had no desire to do so.

He swept a kiss along her cheek and took her hand in his. "What are you two talking about? It feels very tense over here."

"None of your business," Blanche said, exchanging a glance with Jennifer.

"Widow stuff," Jennifer said with a quick smile at Mitch. "They're dancing. Dance with me?"

"Yes, ma'am," he said, and he whisked her several paces away and took her effortlessly into his arms.

Blanche watched them for a turn or two, noting that they did look good together. Jennifer didn't want her to do the stand-up routine simply to torture her, Blanche knew. She wanted her to do it so Blanche would find part of herself again. The part that had always been uniquely hers. The part that had never belonged to Gregory. The part that had not died when he had.

Blanche turned away from the party and made her way to the edge of it, to where a man wearing the maroon blazer and black pants stood. "Sir," she said. "Can you find me Nahvi Samuelson? I need to talk to her."

"Yes, ma'am," he said. "Just a moment."

Blanche took another sip of her wine in the few minutes she waited before Nahvi touched her elbow and said, “You needed me?”

“Yes.” Blanche put down the glass, glad she hadn’t started to buzz with only two tiny sips. “I’ll do the show. Can you take me to the stage and show me what I’m dealing with?”

Nahvi’s smile could’ve lit the yacht for the next week. “Absolutely. Come with me, ma’am. It’ll be in our biggest theater space here, which fits all one hundred guests, the Luxury Lounge.”

Chapter Nine

Jennifer smiled to herself as she sank deeper into Mitch's side. The pool deck wasn't large by any means, but the infinity pool practically hanging over the edge of the yacht offered spectacular swimming, great views, and a romantic spot tucked away from the busyness of the rest of the vessel.

Only six loungers occupied the shady space under the deck above—the last remaining level on the yacht was the Sky Deck, and only a small bar existed up there for guests. A cozy—and coveted—spot beside the pool, and Jennifer and Mitch had lucked into grabbing a single lounger as another man had been leaving.

"Panama Canal tomorrow," she said.

"Mm." Mitch had mentioned wanting to take a nap, and it sounded like he was halfway there. They'd secured their lounger with the snowy white towels handed out by the pool attendant and then enjoyed a dip in the pool.

After toweling off and ordering drinks and appetizers from the café on the other side of the wall where the loungers sat, they'd finally relaxed together on the single seat. She'd faced him while they'd eaten shrimp tacos, and now, it seemed, it was naptime.

"Mitch?" she asked anyway.

His hand tightened along her upper arm. "Hmm?"

She adjusted her sunglasses and looked down the row of other loungers. The other five all held a couple too; no singles here. They held hands and private conversations, and the two attendants—one on either side of the row—looked utterly bored.

"What are you planning to do after this cruise?"

His whole body tensed beside her, and Jennifer felt an electric zing move from his muscles into hers. "I don't understand the question. I'm retired. I don't do anything."

She laughed lightly. "Come on. That's not true." She twisted to look up at him. "Nothing? All day everyday?" She gave him a smile. "Seems like you'd have time to come to Five Island Cove and visit me then."

He smiled in return. "Oh, is that what you were asking? If I'd come visit you?"

"No." She faced the pool and ultimately the ocean again. "I'm asking why we're snuggled up on this lounger together, with half of our cruise left. I'm asking if we're going to get to New York, hug, say we had a great time, and never talk again. I'm asking you what your plans are after this ends."

She was almost seventy years old. She had no more bushes to beat around. Surely Mitch didn't either.

"I live in Jersey," he said. "It's what? A couple of hours to the cove?"

"Probably," she said, though Jennifer knew. She'd gone to the city plenty since Connor had died. The majority of their banking was done there, and sometimes Jennifer simply wanted to be in person for the meetings she had with her financial advisors and wealth management team.

"So either one of us could get to the other easily."

"I have a job," she reminded him. "Remember? Dentist's office? Gotta keep those patients happy, with clean teeth." She smiled, though she didn't need the job. She did it because it gave her something to do, and it kept up appearances that she wasn't the millionaire next door.

"Yes," he murmured, his lips very close to her ear. "I think you have a secret about that dentist job."

"Do I?" She could flirt if she had to, and Mitch's chuckle told her she'd done a good job of it.

"You said you did," he said. "Wouldn't tell me what it was...yet."

Jennifer pressed her lips together. She was a very good secret-keeper. She always had been, but she'd seen the damage her tight-lipped nature could cause. "Okay." She took a deep breath. "I don't need the dentist job. I do it, because people expect me to have something coming in to help pay my bills."

Mitch said nothing, and Jennifer adjusted the skirt on her swimming suit so it covered more of her thigh.

"I don't need the money. My husband left me plenty of money, but...no one knows that."

"Ah." He got the picture without her having to connect all the dots for him.

"Not even Robin—until recently," she said. "We're going to get together and go through things, though. When I get back to the cove." She glanced up to Mitch again, then quickly away. He was so bright, and she couldn't hold his gaze for long. He wore no sunglasses, and his white hair swooped to the right now that it had gotten wet and started to dry. He was a stunningly handsome man, and Jennifer let herself sink into the warmth the two of them created.

Several long seconds went by, wherein Jennifer allowed her eyelids to flutter closed. Then Mitch murmured, "I was thinking I'd like to see if this can be more than fifteen days."

Jennifer's eyes snapped open again. "You were?"

"What are you going to do when you get home?" he asked.

She knew he didn't mean check-in dental patients and pretend she didn't have money.

"That's my secret," he said. "Now I know one of yours and you know one of mine."

She nudged him gently with her elbow. "That's not a secret. I told you a real one."

He chuckled, the sound low, deep, and rumbling

with magic. "I suppose we'll have to keep seeing each other so I can tell you all of mine."

"Start with an easy one," she insisted, though she did like the things he'd been saying.

"Okay." He cleared his throat. "If you'll tell me why Blanche has been acting cagey today."

Jennifer stiffened this time. "I don't know what you mean."

"You do too. You two were conspiring about something at the cocktail party last night."

"That is not true." Jennifer sat up slightly and turned to look at him again. "We were talking about our dead husbands. Nothing nefarious about it at all."

Mitch blinked once. "I know she's hiding something from me."

"That's between the two of you then."

His eyes searched hers; he even reached up and removed her sunglasses so they could make true eye contact. Jennifer would not tell him anything about Blanche's comedy sketch that night. She'd awakened to a text from her friend that said she'd accepted the offer to do her routine, and the cruise line would be sending out a notification to the app that day.

Mitch lived and died by the notifications on his Silver Sails app, but he hadn't gotten anything yet. Plenty of daylight still stretched in front of them, and Jennifer suddenly knew what she wanted to do with it.

He continued to watch her, silently, and she knew why it bothered Blanche. It didn't annoy her, however, because he wasn't judging her. His eyes held a softness that said his feelings for her were real, and a surge of emotion reared up inside Jennifer.

He leaned in slightly, which kicked up her heart rate, and asked, "What are you thinking?"

Jennifer smiled, a slow expression that made his smile appear and widen too. She didn't answer his question directly, because while she was no-nonsense in business, she'd been rusty in love for a long, long time. "Do you want to do something with the time we have left?"

"Absolutely," he whispered without missing a beat.

She tilted her head back ever so slightly before murmuring, "This." She pressed her lips to his, hoping there weren't too many eyes on them. The loungers almost existed in bubbles of their own, and they hadn't been interrupted by anyone, passenger or crew, since arriving on the deck over an hour ago.

The kiss was gentle at first; hesitant even, as if neither one of them wanted to move too far or too fast. But as the seconds passed by, he grew bolder, deepening the kiss and sliding his hand along Jennifer's throat.

She savored the taste and touch of him, letting herself do what she'd been doing for the past eight days on this cruise—get lost. Lost inside her head. Lost in the beauty of riding a horse through Mexico. Lost in the Costa Rica jungle.

Completely lost in this beautiful kiss with this beautiful man.

When they finally pulled apart, Jennifer couldn't

seem to get a full breath. Heat assaulted her face, and she realized she'd reached up and threaded her fingers through Mitch's hair too.

Their eyes met, and she didn't duck her head. Or giggle. Or let any embarrassment creep in. She wasn't embarrassed. She was old enough to kiss a man and mean it, and she didn't have to apologize to anyone about it.

Mitch carried a hint of ruddiness in his face too, and he said, "Good?"

"Mm." Very good. "Let's see if the second time is as good as the first."

He chuckled and leaned down to kiss her again. Sparks popped along her skin, and she paid more attention to where her hands went this time. His too.

"Mitch?"

He broke the kiss quickly, turning away from Jennifer and almost trying to shield her at the same time. That would never work, for they were entangled together on a single lounge chair.

Blanche stood there, gaping. She gathered herself together in the wake of silence that seemed to pulse around them. She folded her arms and cocked one hip. "You big fat liar."

"I am not a liar," Mitch said in a dignified voice.

"You told me you weren't spending the night with her."

"I'm not." He glanced over to Jennifer, his thoughts as plain as the sunshine surrounding them. He wanted to, a fact that made Jennifer feel fifty years younger. She wasn't sure that would happen anytime soon, but it was nice to be wanted.

He shifted, and Jennifer moved to get to her feet. Her phone buzzed beneath her thigh as she did, indicating she had a text or a call she'd missed. Honestly, the world had disappeared during that kiss.

She picked up her phone and saw it was the cruise line, notifying her of a change in the schedule for that evening. "Oh." Her eyes flew to Blanche's, searching now. "He's about to find out."

"I came to tell him," she said. "Right when they sent it out. I suppose I should be glad he was...preoccupied."

"Tell me what?" Mitch also got to his feet, but he'd stowed his phone in Jennifer's bag. Her eyes dropped to it, and Blanche's followed.

She moved to stand more in front of the bag, as if Mitch would lunge for it and retrieve his phone before she could tell him about her comedy show.

Voices behind her made their way into Jennifer's ears, and she distinctly heard, "That's her right there."

And, "Who knew we were on the yacht with someone famous?"

Mitch heard them too. He looked over to the couple next to them and back to Blanche.

"I'm doing my act," she said in the blunt way she had. "Tonight, here on the ship."

His eyebrows went up. He opened his mouth, and in true Mitch-fashion, he said. "Blanche, that's great news," just before he wrapped his sister in a big, brotherly hug.

Jennifer watched the way Blanche's eyes drifted closed. The broadness of her smile. The way she held her brother back. The pure joy and comfort and way they clearly knew each other so well.

She had absolutely no one like that, and she missed that connection. A well of deep longing opened inside her, one she'd covered with as many defenses as she could.

It hadn't dried up. It hadn't gone away. She'd simply hidden it for a time.

Now, watching Mitch murmur something to Blanche, and seeing how she nodded and then wiped her eyes, Jennifer wanted a relationship with someone that didn't have any secrets in it. No mystery. No intrigue.

Just acceptance. Belonging. Peace. The ability to be herself, and still be loved anyway.

Mitch turned back to her and laced his fingers through hers, making her wonder if he could be the man to love her, flaws and all.

Maybe, a voice whispered. *If you let him in and erase all the secrets between you.*

Chapter Ten

Watching Blanche on-stage filled Jennifer with pride and joy. The woman knew exactly how to charm a crowd, and she knew exactly who she was speaking to. The crowd sixty and older liked jokes told a certain way, and she'd prepared an entire set on things from the past that only their generation would understand.

Her mind walked down paths Jennifer's never would, and she hadn't laughed as hard as she had in the past thirty minutes in a very long time. When Blanche said, "And that's why, folks, you simply need a rotary phone," tying her last punch line to one of her earlier jokes, the crowd went wild, whooping and whistling, the applause almost deafening in the Luxury Lounge.

Jennifer sprang to her feet, only half a second behind Mitch, the two of them yelling and clapping for Blanche.

She put her microphone back in the stand and bowed from the waist before lifting both hands up and waving to the other ninety-nine passengers on-board. Well, Jennifer didn't know if they'd all come tonight, but word of this amazing show would spread like wildfire on this small boat, and the lounge would be packed tomorrow for sure.

Jennifer kept clapping until her friend walked off stage, at which point, the applause finally started to die down. She turned to Mitch, almost as breathless now as she'd been after their first kiss earlier that day.

"She was incredible." She turned to make sure she hadn't left her phone or her drink behind. The drink was gone, and her phone sat tucked into her shorts pocket. "Right?"

"Simply incredible," Mitch said. "Let's go see if she'll have a nightcap with us." He took Jennifer's hand and moved into the aisle. People had already flooded it, and moving out of the lounge would take several minutes.

"She won't," Jennifer said. "She told you that at dinner. She's not going to come out and talk to people afterward, including us."

"She's so stubborn," Mitch said.

"She is who she is." Jennifer looked at him then, glad when he met her eye. He seemed to slow down then, and he nodded.

"You're right. I don't know why I'm trying to change her after all these years."

"She doesn't need to be changed," Jennifer said. "She needs you to accept her for who she is. Love her for it."

"I do love her," Mitch said, frowning. "We've lived near each other our whole lives. We've been there for each other through everything."

"And yet, you're still trying to inflict your will onto her."

"You have no idea what I'm doing." His hand tightened along hers and then let go.

The loss of it cascaded through her. The stubborn part of her wanted to throw up walls with thick bricks and plenty of mortar between them. Instead, she said, "I'm sorry. I didn't mean it to sound like you were doing something wrong. I don't know everything about your relationship with your sister."

He nodded, but he didn't take her hand again. Beyond the Luxury Lounge, twilight was just beginning to fade into dusk. Dinner lasted from four-thirty to seven, with the shows and evening activities beginning immediately afterward. Nothing went past nine o'clock, but a single bar remained open until eleven.

Jennifer hadn't frequented it during these first nine days on the yacht, and she wouldn't tonight either. She needed her rest for the Panama Canal tomorrow, and then a stop in Colombia the next day. Simply talking, dining, and attending a few activities each day was more interaction and activity than she normally did.

Mitch loved to sip wine in the evening, and he had

stayed out on her balcony until very late one night. *One* night. They'd sipped and whispered and listened to the ocean on the other nights, but he'd retired about ten-thirty, when she really started yawning.

So he wasn't trying to change her.

She slipped her hand back into Mitch's. "Let's see if we can tell her congratulations in person, and then let's get a glass of wine and head to my suite."

He looked at her, new questions in his eyes since their kiss that day. Jennifer simply smiled, because she wasn't sure what the night might hold. Her suite was the only one at the back of the ship on her deck. She shared walls with no other room, with a suite identical to hers across the hall both laterally and toward the bow of the ship.

Not that she'd do anything too loud with Mitch that night. She wasn't really the type to do that. Her love-making with Connor had been serene almost. Passionate, yes. But tame. She didn't need a rough tumble in the sheets. She wanted a man to look at her in such a way that his love for her could be seen and felt before he even touched her.

It had been far too long since Jennifer had felt like that with a man. Sex was nothing to her; she wanted *love*. And she knew that Mitch didn't love her. How could he? After only eight days and a few kisses? They'd shared a few things about their lives, sure, but not enough to truly form a bond that spelled love.

Perhaps the beginnings of it, sure. She'd admit that. A solid framework on which they could continue to build their relationship.

They waited, but Blanche didn't come out. After ten minutes, Mitch admitted defeat and texted his sister. Then he pocketed his phone and said, "Red wine tonight? Or white?"

She smiled at him and placed one hand against his chest. "What do you think?"

"I think if I come back to your room with white wine, you'll kick me to the curb." He grinned too and led her toward the stairs. They went up a couple of decks to the main dining level, and Mitch got a bottle of the delicious red wine that they'd been enjoying for the past several evenings.

It would take them at least two nights to drink it all, perhaps even three, but Jennifer had a wine fridge in her room, so she could chill whatever they didn't consume tonight.

Back in her room, she kicked off her low heels with a sigh. Mitch closed and locked the door behind her, and he busied himself with pouring the wine. He turned toward her and extended one of the glasses, and Jennifer took it.

She didn't take a sip though. Something wild rose up within her, and she set her glass on the narrow nightstand where her phone charger lay. "Mitch," she said.

He took a sip of his wine and swirled the deep, ruby

liquid in his glass, his eyes on it instead of her. When he finally looked at her, nothing else needed to be said. He wrapped one arm around her and brought her to his chest in one fluid move.

"I'm not going to spend the night." He kissed her before she could answer, and Jennifer didn't know what she wanted. She did see and feel things in Mitch's expression she hadn't seen or felt in a while.

He somehow got rid of his wine glass. He kept his hands up around her face and neck as he kissed her, and Jennifer kissed him back. Mitch's touch was gentle and exploratory, as if he were afraid that she'd pull away. When he finally broke the kiss, his eyes filled with an emotion Jennifer couldn't place. He seemed to be asking her something she didn't understand.

"Let's go sit outside," he said. He took her hand in one of his and his wine in the other and led her outside.

They sat in the dusk until it became darkness, the silence between them comfortable and even peaceful. Jennifer didn't know what to say, because she'd asked him what his plans were post-cruise, and they both now knew their feelings for each other had strength.

She finally said, "I'm going to call Stu once we go through the canal."

"Sounds like a good plan." He looked over to her. "I should call my kids too. Let them know I'm still alive." He smiled and finished his wine before he stood. "I'm going to head to bed, sweetheart. Do you want me to tuck you in?"

She shook her head. "I'm going to sit out here for a while longer." She gestured to the pure blackness in front of her. "Listen to her for a while."

"All right." He bent down and kissed her, and Jennifer tipped her head back to receive him more easily. "Good night, gorgeous."

He left, and Jennifer finished her first glass of wine too, listening to the sound of the sea and letting it infuse into her in a way nothing else could. She couldn't understand the ocean's language, but she knew how it made her feel—how it had always made her feel.

Loved.

Now, she simply needed to find a way to mend the broken bridges between her and her son.

"After the Panama Canal," she whispered, a promise to herself...and the sea.

JENNIFER STOOD AT THE BOW OF THE YACHT, along with nearly everyone else on-board. They'd been told via the app that the front of the vessel, on the Panorama Deck or the Coastal Deck, would have the best views of the Panama Canal as they moved through it.

She stood with Mitch's hand resting lightly on her hip, him on her left, with Blanche on her right. "This is incredible," she gushed. "I've never done anything like this." She and Connor had never traveled all that much. Even now, she barely left the cove.

Blanche had said she'd traveled all over North America doing comedy shows, but even she seemed raptly attune to the yacht as it moved into the first lock. "It's only a ten-foot clearance on the sides. Incredible."

"The water will raise us fifty-four feet," a man said over the loudspeaker on-board the yacht. "To Lake Miraflores. This takes about an hour or so. Oh, the gates are opening."

The gates, he'd already explained were huge, thick, and took about ten minutes just to open. The water wasn't blue and tropical like out in the ocean, but a deep, muddy, greenish-brown.

Row upon row of people stood in a viewing area, and Jennifer could see a visitor's center above them as well. The waterway was black until about halfway up, then it turned into what looked like rust-stained cement. The lock doors were black and thick and iron as they started to open. She almost expected a rushing of water to come spilling out of them, but it didn't.

The yacht had been taken over by a Panama Canal Captain, as they were the only people allowed to sail a vessel through the canal. The trip from Pacific Ocean to Atlantic would take all day, roughly eight to ten hours, and they'd already been told they'd be having lunch on Gatan Lake.

"I recommend doing a two-day tour of the Panama Canal one day," the announcer said now. "If you ever come back this way. You can take boats out into the rain forests of Gatan Lake, which is simply beautiful."

Jennifer looked from Blanche to Mitch, and it was almost an unspoken pact the three of them made in that moment. She definitely wanted to come back to this part of the world and explore it more. She reached over and squeezed Blanche's hand.

"Your show last night was incredible," she said quietly. She'd texted Blanche too, but this was the first time she'd seen her in person since the show.

"Thank you," she said. "I rewrote some of the jokes and put in some new ones, so the show won't be a complete repeat from last night."

Jennifer nodded as the PA crackled to life again. "The doors are open, and we'll be moving in slowly in a minute. Then, once the doors are securely closed behind us, the water will start to rise, lifting us to the level of the next lock."

It was a slow process, but one of complete engineering genius. Jennifer marveled that people could build something like this; that someone had even thought of it in the first place.

Their yacht slowly moved from south to north, from the Pacific Ocean to the Caribbean Sea. The title of the app notification kept running through her head.

One Day, Two Oceans, Three Locks.

The Gatan lock was the last one, and by the time they reached Lake Gatan and only had that one lock system left to traverse, Jennifer's stomach cried for food. Her feet told her to find somewhere to sit, and she was ready to stop being gawked at. Plenty of people had been pointing too.

She'd taken pictures of the locks, of the scenery on both sides, and of every wildlife sighting someone or the announcer had pointed out.

Mantled howler monkeys, and white-faced capuchin monkeys, and even a yellow-throated toucan. The wildlife seemed to shift and vary as the day wore on, which made sense, as they were literally moving from one climate to another. Going over hills and mountains that would be impossible for the water to do without the lock system.

Lake Gatan held a sense of serenity that Jennifer craved in her own life, and she leaned against the railing and smiled. Many people had left to get lunch, so there was more breathing and standing room on the deck, and Jennifer let the Panama breeze welcome her to its country.

"This is a fresh-water lake," a man said beside her, and she turned to look at him. "When the locks open, the fresh water mixes with the salt water, and it'll create a mottled, swirling appearance. Almost like gasoline on water."

"Interesting," she said, and she meant it. "The Bridge of the Americas was beautiful, wasn't it?"

"I got a picture for my son." The man pulled out his phone and tapped, swiped, and then turned the device toward her. He stood in the picture, the glorious bridge spanning the scene behind him. The black arch lifted above his head, and Jennifer couldn't help smiling at it again.

"That's amazing." She'd only taken a picture of the bridge itself, not one with her in it. Robin always told her pictures were better with people in them, but Jennifer rarely wanted to take a selfie just to get a picture of a bridge.

"I think it's fascinating how much the climate has changed."

"I wasn't expecting that either," he said. "I sort of thought it would be a straight shot from east to west." He chuckled, and Jennifer laughed lightly with him.

"It's not even east to west."

A cry rose up from the other side of the boat, and they both turned that way. Mitch and Blanche had eased over to another position, and Jennifer found Mitch turning toward her, motioning her forward with an urgent look on his face.

She hurried to his side. "What is it?"

"A three-toed sloth." He pointed toward the forest that crept right up to the edge of the water. "Look. Can you see it on that tree there?"

She searched, a desperation rising up within her. A sloth! She wanted to see that. All at once, her eyes landed on it. "Oh, my goodness." Jennifer pressed one hand to her chest, beyond glad she'd come on this cruise.

She quickly handed her phone to Mitch. "Take my picture with it, would you?" She wasn't the only one posing to get themselves in a picture with the sloth, and

Mitch took one of her, then one of her and Blanche, and then a selfie with the three of them.

"He's one famous sloth," Blanche quipped, and then she cracked a grin. "I bet I can work him into a joke tonight."

"I bet you can," Jennifer said with a smile. She watched the sloth until she couldn't see it anymore, a thread of happiness pulling through her that she hadn't truly felt before. Her life in Five Island Cove was a good one, of course. But having experiences like this reminded her that the world was a big place. Money didn't mean as much as she sometimes thought it did. And having a personal connection with the right people meant more to her than she'd previously realized.

They'd come up eighty-five feet in sea level to get to this lake and get across the Panama isthmus. They had eighty-five feet—and hours—to go to get to the other side and on their way again. Each one felt like a triumph to Jennifer, and they each served as a reminder that nothing could truly be done in one straight shot.

She had to work in steps and locks with her children. It hadn't taken one argument or one disagreement to get them to where they were. She could make amends one foot at a time, opening the heavy doors to her life and her heart until they were splayed wide open and she could let her children back in.

"Come on," Mitch said. "If we don't go eat soon, we'll miss lunch."

Jennifer's stomach growled, and she didn't want to

miss lunch, but she said, "Let me text this picture to my kids really quick first."

She did that while her friends waited, and only then did she look up, more hopeful and feeling more happiness and more gratitude than she ever had. "Okay, ready."

Chapter Eleven

Blanche put the last bite of her delicious steak in her mouth, her stomach way too full to hold it. She'd eaten it anyway, because it had been one of the best meals of her life. She pressed her eyes closed, enjoying the juicy meat with just the right amount of salt and pepper, the way it melted in her mouth, and the slight film of fat it left on her lips.

"I love this restaurant," she said aloud to the other five people at her table. "I think it'll be the thing I miss most about being on the cruise." She smiled around at them. "What will you miss the most?"

She'd been seated with three other singles and a couple tonight, without Mitch or Jennifer as her wing-men. Her comedy routines the past two nights had given her more confidence than she knew she'd lost, and tomorrow, they'd dock at the port in Colombia. The alert to sign up for excursions had come in the mid-afternoon, and Blanche had booked herself a ticket to the Emerald Museum, with a visit to some of the older places in the area. A fortress she'd forgotten the name of and the old walled city of Cartagena.

She loved ruins and old things, exploring things that had long passed from glory, and it had sounded like the perfect excursion for her. She hadn't asked Jennifer or Mitch to go with her, and when her brother had texted her to find out her plans, Blanche had said she'd made her own.

She didn't want to admit that he'd been right about bringing her on this cruise, but...he'd been right. She'd needed to get outside the radius of where she and Gregory had lived for the past fifty years, and this fifteen-day adventure from country to country, climate to climate, had done that.

She'd never seen anything like the Panama Canal in her whole life, and she hadn't realized how desperately she'd needed a master engineer in her life to lift and lower the water until it was exactly the right level to let her pass through.

A man named Richard gave her a smile. "I think I'm going to miss the fact that someone else makes my meals, no matter what they are."

"I agree there," she said.

"I'm not much of a cook." He looked to the woman seated next to him. "What about you?"

"I'm from Edmonton," she said. "Canada. I'm going

to miss the ocean." She sighed wistfully. "It's so bright and beautiful. We don't see anything like this where I'm from."

Around the table they went, until they'd returned to Blanche. She smiled and nodded and agreed with all of them. The food. The view. The perfectly made beds in the morning. The poker nights. Someone had even said her show was something they'd enjoyed immensely and would miss.

She glanced at her phone, noting the time. "I have to leave a few minutes early," she said. "Someone enjoy my dessert for me."

"Good luck tonight," chorused from the others, and Blanche's heart swelled with love for them. With so few passengers on the ship, she'd seen all of their faces before, it being day eleven of their time together, and she smiled and nodded her way out of the Italian bistro that served seriously delicious wagyu beef.

Once in the hallway, she nearly smacked into a man she'd seen several times. She'd eaten with him twice now, and she said, "Oh, I'm sorry, Frank. I didn't see you."

"On the way to the Luxury Lounge?" he asked as she patted down her hair and smoothed her blouse.

Their eyes met, and Blanche nodded. "Yes. I have to be backstage in a few minutes."

"Can I walk with you?" He eyed the restaurant, his stomach making a very loud growl. She looked down at his midsection and grinned.

"You haven't eaten dinner yet."

"I have the last time slot," he admitted.

"If you walk with me, you'll miss it." She raised her eyebrows, asking him silently if he wanted to skip dinner.

He gestured her down the hall. "I don't feel like socializing tonight."

"You don't?" He'd been one of the more social men on the cruise. He hadn't paired off with anyone that she'd noticed, but Blanche had stopped paying attention days ago.

Frank shook his head, his salt-and-pepper hair flopping slightly with the movement. Blanche stepped in front of him and preceded him down the hallway. "Can I ask why not?"

"I—" He cut off, and it wasn't until they'd entered the elevator—after a giggling couple who acted like they were fifteen instead of sixty-five stepped off—that he continued. "My wife passed away only a year ago." He cleared his throat. "Today."

Instant empathy overcame Blanche. For a reason she couldn't name, tears filled her eyes. She reached out and took Frank's hand in hers. There was no spark there. She wasn't sure she'd ever be ready for another relationship. But she was this man's friend, and he needed her. She needed him.

"I'm so sorry, Frank. I can't even imagine what a mess I'll be on the anniversary of my husband's death."

His fingers wrapped warmly around hers. "How long has it been?" he asked in a whisper.

"Only nine months." The words practically choked her as she said them. She couldn't let herself go down this rabbit hole right now. She had to be peppy and ready to crack jokes in only a half-hour.

"You'll call me," he said, his face brightening with a smile. "And we'll just talk. It won't be too bad, I promise."

"Is that what you've done today? Talk to people?"

"Mostly her," he admitted. "From my balcony or the Sky Deck. I feel her close to me, but I can also feel her moving...away." A wistful look entered his eyes. "I can't describe it. She's close, but she's leaving." He met Blanche's eyes again. "I don't want her to leave." He swallowed, but no tears fell from his eyes.

She didn't know what to say to comfort him. Had the roles been reversed, she wouldn't want someone to say anything to her. She'd just want them to be there. She just wanted someone to hear her. She just didn't want to feel so alone.

"I understand," she whispered. The doors to the elevator slid open, and of course she'd come face-to-face with her brother. Mitch's face registered surprise, then a smile. No one moved, and his eyes dropped to where Blanche's hand connected to Frank's.

His eyebrows practically flew off his forehead then, and he bullied his way onto the elevator instead of letting the pair of them off first. "What's going on in here?"

"Nothing," Blanche said, puffing out her chest.

"You're supposed to let the people off the elevator before you get on." She side-stepped him, dropping Frank's hand.

"You'll be great tonight," he said. "I have a water-painting class, or I'd come."

"Thank you, Frank," she said. "See you later." She started to walk away, hoping the man could handle her older brother on the anniversary of his wife's death. Suddenly, she sucked in a breath and turned back.

She caught the elevator doors just as they started to close. "Mitch," she said. "Do not question him about anything."

"He's a grown man," Mitch said darkly. "He can answer why he was holding my sister's hand in the elevator."

Frank looked between the two of them. "It was nothing," he said quickly.

"His wife died today," Blanche said, shooting him an apologetic look. "A year ago. It was a comforting thing; nothing serious."

Mitch's whole demeanor changed as Frank said, "Your sister is a very good listener." He gave her a small smile. "I do hope we can keep talking after the cruise, but there's nothing...too romantic there."

Blanche felt oddly reassured that he'd felt the same kindling of friendship for her that she'd experienced for him. She met her brother's eyes again. "Okay? Be nice to him. Nothing's going on."

Mitch nodded, and Blanche backed out of the

elevator as it started to squeal. "Oops," she said with a grin as wide as the Panama Canal they'd just traversed yesterday. "Sorry." She laughed as she walked away from the elevator, whose door wouldn't close at all now. It finally did, amidst her brother's sour words, and Blanche steeled herself to get on stage and tell jokes.

She shook out her hands, which somehow had always allowed the nerves to flee and her best performances to come forth.

Throwback comedy tonight. Emeralds tomorrow.

The next morning, Blanche packed her backpack with sunscreen and two of the cans of water she got every morning in her room. She hadn't been drinking them both each day, so she had a stockpile. A river of nerves ran through her, but she straightened and mentally went through her checklist again.

She'd get fed on today's excursion, so she didn't need food. She'd packed one of her favorite granola bars anyway, knowing she'd like the pumpkin seeds and dark chocolate with a hint of sea salt by mid-morning.

She had a lightweight windbreaker, though they'd left the colder Pacific side of the continent in favor of the more tropical Caribbean side. Sunscreen, water, and her thread wallet, should she want to purchase anything in Colombia today.

Packed and ready, she threw back the last of her

protein shake, shouldered her pack, and left her cabin. Several other folks waited for the elevator, and Blanche opted to take the stairs instead. She made her way alone toward the exit, as the ship had pulled up to the dock about an hour ago.

Even before she disembarked, she saw the woman holding the bright green sign for the Emerald Museum, and to her great delight—not—two couples waited with her. Blanche told herself that no matter who else showed up, they'd be a single. She wouldn't be the only one.

"Unless there are only five of you," she muttered to herself. The only thing worse than being a third wheel was a fifth wheel, and Blanche steeled herself for that possibility as she waited her turn to leave the walkway connecting yacht to land.

She joined the crew waiting for the Emerald Museum and gave the woman her name. "I'm Nathalia. I'll be your guide today. One more." She looked back to the ship. "We're just waiting on one more."

"Who is it?" Blanche asked.

"Uh...Mister Frank Bellasi," Nathalia said.

"Oh, Frank," Blanche said, her whole day getting brighter. Not only would she not be the only singleton on this excursion today, she'd be with a friend. "I know Frank." She said it like he was the President of the United States and she, his close, personal advisor.

The two couples simply smiled at her, and a moment later, she caught sight of Frank weaving through the crowd toward them. "Sorry," he said somewhat breathlessly, barely looking at Blanche. "I didn't mean to be late. I had a plumbing mishap in my room." He tightened the straps on his backpack and looked at Nathalia

She checked him in, and as Frank slowed down, he took in the people standing there. "Blanche," he said pleasantly.

"Ah, so now you see me." She gave him a wide smile and let him brush his lips along her cheek. "A plumbing mishap?"

"Come with me," Nathalia said. "Our van is over here." She set out, away from the dock and the other groups still gathering, and Blanche followed her.

"My sink spurted water everywhere," he said. "I had to change my clothes, call someone, and try to keep the water from overflowing, all at the same time." He shook his head. "I'm still praying I won't return tonight to an *underwater* suite."

Blanche grinned at him as another man in the group said, "I hope you don't too. Was anyone there to help when you left?"

"Yes," Frank said. "And I'd used all my available towels soaking up the water." He shook his head. "I'm still giving this cruise five stars, but only if they provide another swimming suit if my suite is soaked when we get back." He seemed much more upbeat today, and he knew one of the couples in the group. Suddenly, it was the four of them, with the other couple on the outside. Blanche knew that feeling—she often felt outside her own family group now that Gregory was gone—so she made sure to start a conversation with them too.

"How many of you have seen Romancing the Stone?" Nathalia asked, now standing at the front of the van. Blanche had taken a seat right in the middle of it, and the chatter quieted as they all looked up to their guide.

She had, so she raised her hand.

"They were looking for an emerald," Nathalia said, her eyes shining like the gems. She wore a pretty smile too. "And while they used a prop in the movie, they based it on one of the largest emeralds in the world—and that came straight from the mines here in Colombia." She spoke with an accent, but her English was impeccable.

"Now, they didn't film the movie here—it happened mostly in Mexico—but our emerald experts provided consultations throughout the making of the movie. Today, you're going to get to see how we process emeralds in our Emerald Museum. You'll get to see some of the oldest parts of Colombia, with some rich history and plenty of surprises. Our first one." She grabbed onto the back of the driver's seat as he gunned the engine and she nearly got thrown out the back window.

"Postre de Natas." She beamed as she held up a pitcher of what looked like a yellower version of milk. Very thick, yellow milk. "We'll be sampling a variety of Colombian treats and sweets and foods today, especially once we leave the museum. But how many of you like coffee?"

Once again, every hand went up. "Postre de Natas isn't anything like that." Nathalia giggled and continued with, "It's a creamy, milk pudding. Sometimes, if you're feeling a little naughty, you can put rum in it."

She began to pour the thick pudding into clear plastic cups. How she managed the feat while staying on her feet as the driver zipped around the Colombian streets, Blanche would never know. A task for a younger woman, she supposed.

"There's no rum in this today," she said. "We also leave out the raisins for our tour groups, but you can add them."

"Sort of like rice pudding," a man in the back said.

"Yes," Nathalia said without missing a beat. "It's traditionally a desert, but again, if you're feeling naughty..." She tipped her cup back and took a swallow of the pudding. "You eat it for breakfast."

Blanche raised her cup to Frank, and he knocked his plastic against hers. "Pudding for breakfast," she said.

"Pudding for Christmas breakfast," he repeated.

"Merry Christmas." She'd actually forgotten it was Christmas Day. Now that she thought about it, she'd seen wreaths and red ribbons on the ship, but they hadn't registered in her head.

She'd brought a small gift for Mitch, which she'd give him later, and that was all. With Frank waiting, she took a drink, finding it sweeter than she'd thought. And a little mapley, which surprised her too. “Oh, it’s good.” She hoped it would be the very sweet start to a very good day.

As the tour got started, she took out her phone and set a reminder to call her girls later that evening, once she’d returned to the yacht. After all, it was Christmas.

Then she lifted her Christmas pudding drink to her lips again and took another sip.

Chapter Twelve

Jennifer flipped her phone over and over in her hand, sure it would slip from her fingers at any moment. The morning light hadn't turned golden yet, and her balcony existed in shades of gray. If she edged just a little closer to the railing, if she accidentally dropped her phone, it would splash into the ocean.

They'd left Colombia last night, and after another full day of cruising, they'd arrive in Grand Cayman. Today was a "down day" according to the Silver Sails app. A brunch buffet would be served instead of lunch, and the afternoon activities included knitting, trivia games, bunko, aerial meditation, and several movies.

She needed a relaxing day after the highs of going through the Panama Canal and then exploring the beauty of Colombia. She and Blanche were meeting later today to talk about money, something Jennifer was actually really looking forward to.

She'd felt several things unlock inside her since boarding this yacht, and finally learning how to loosen her grip on the millions she had in the bank felt like that last clasp that needed to be unbuckled.

On the other hand, Blanche needed to pull back on her spending, and Jennifer felt like they existed on opposite ends of the spectrum and could help balance each other a little.

She wasn't planning to see Mitch until brunch, and her window to call her son shrank with every flip of her phone.

Stu would be up and getting ready to leave for work. He and his family lived in Brooklyn, and he commuted into the city for his job each day. He had a daughter who'd graduated a few years ago, but she hadn't gone to college. Jennifer wasn't sure what Eva was doing now, as she hadn't spoken to her son in a while.

His wife, Anna-Maria, made and ran an online jewelry business that kept her busy and filled a whole bedroom in their modest apartment. Jennifer had her opinions about Stu's choices, but she'd realized too late that she didn't have to say them out loud.

She'd sent him the picture of her and the three-toed sloth, but he hadn't responded. She'd hoped he might if it was a group text with his sister. Robin had, and several texts had been exchanged between the two of them.

Stu had remained silent.

Jennifer flipped her phone and swiped it on. She

tapped to get to the messages and scrolled back through them.

Mom, that's amazing! Robin had said. *Have you seen a lot of wildlife on the cruise?*

Birds, mostly. But the Panama Canal is amazing. We have to come, all of us. She remembered the nerves that had pinged through her stomach as she'd sent that text. She had not given her children much of anything since Connor's death. They were adults. They'd both been married, with jobs and spouses with jobs.

When Connor had been alive, they hadn't taken family vacations. That hadn't changed after his death, but Jennifer wanted to do something different now. Bridges were built one plank at a time. One support.

The engineering feats she'd seen in the bridges and locks in the Panama Canal had shown her that seemingly impossible things could be achieved.

She could call her son. It simply *felt* impossible; it wasn't actually.

Jennifer tapped her son's name and then the phone icon. His number came up, the bright green circle the only thing standing between her and making the telephone call. She took a breath and tapped it, and the line started to connect.

She lifted the phone to her ear and slowly released her breath one measure at a time. Surely Stu hadn't blocked her number, so he'd know it was her calling. Would he be too busy to pick up? Or would he simply ignore her?

The line rang three times, then four. Her heartbeat

pounded like a big steel drum, the reverberations from it vibrating every vein in her body.

Just when she thought the call would go to voicemail and she'd have to leave a falsely cheery message—again—he said, "Mom? Can you hear me?"

"Stuart." She breathed out his full name, shock and relief coursing through her. "I can hear you."

"There you are," he said. Absolutely no emotion rode in his voice, and he didn't offer anything more.

Jennifer suddenly didn't know what to say. Her eyes welled with tears, and she didn't want to speak with so much emotion coursing through her. At the same time, a quiet voice in her head urged her to show her son that his mother was a real person.

"I'm so sorry," she managed to choke out. Her voice sounded like she'd inhaled helium, and the last syllable cracked. "I didn't mean to drive a wedge between us with thoughtless words."

"Mom." Stu sighed, and Jennifer could never tell him how good it felt to hear him call her his mother.

"It's none of my business how you raise Eva. She's an adult now." She took a deep breath through her nose. "She's a lovely young woman. I miss you and the kids. Anna-Maria." She hadn't particularly agreed with Stu's choice in a wife, but he and Anna-Maria had been married for over twenty-five years now. They'd worked together, raised three children, and managed to stay married. That deserved some praise. Some mighty praise indeed.

And yet, all Jennifer had done over the past couple of years was criticize the two of them. She'd lied to her daughter too, about something stupid too. Crab legs. Why she'd done that, Jennifer still didn't know.

She'd put blocks between the two of them with silence and refusals to answer questions, with critical glances at the new house she and Duke had bought, and by constantly talking about Eva and how wonderful she was—when really, Jennifer disapproved of some of her granddaughter's choices too.

"I'm on a cruise," she said. "I'm sure Robin told you. I sent you that picture of the sloth."

"Yeah," Stu said quietly.

Jennifer ignored the stab of hurt at his silence, and kept going. "There's only four more days on the cruise," she said. "We'll be docking in New York City on the morning of December thirtieth. I was hoping..." She trailed off, because her son had said very little. He hadn't accepted her apology. He hadn't given her any indication that he wanted to forgive her and try to have a relationship.

She steeled herself and squared her shoulders. The sun had continued to rise, turning the gray to blue and now gold. The warm rays of it gave her additional courage, and she told herself she'd dealt with plenty of businessmen exactly like her son. She'd put them in their place; she'd presented figures contrary to theirs; she'd sat at the head of the table in plenty of board meetings.

"I was hoping you and the kids would come," she

said. "Robin and Duke are planning to be there. We could go to breakfast in the city. Nothing major."

Just this phone call was major, in her book.

"I'll talk to Anna," Stu said. "The boys should be able to come, since there's no school."

Jennifer nodded, more relief painting through her. She didn't dare ask about Eva. Anna-Maria was particularly sensitive about her daughter, and Jennifer had burned so many bridges with her comments about how the girl dressed, how many piercings she had, and what she should be doing with her life.

In Jennifer's opinion, which she'd learned no one in her family wanted to hear. She'd never felt so isolated as she had in the past couple of years, and she couldn't believe she'd let her stubbornness keep these wedges between her and her children.

She pictured her handsome husband in her mind as she pressed her eyes closed. Connor had told her the day before he'd died to not let her stubbornness dictate her choices. She'd managed to do it for a lot of years, but the past two or three had been driven by a woman motivated only by money.

When was enough enough?

"If you can," she said as she opened her eyes. "I'd love to go out with just you and Robin too. There are a few things I need to..." She cleared her throat. "Discuss with the two of you." She wasn't going to be around forever, and she needed her children to know what she'd continued to build and cultivate after their dad's death.

"We'll see," Stu said.

"Stu." Jennifer felt like she was about to lose him again. "I'm sorry. Please, just know how sorry I am."

"I hear you, Mom," he said. "You're docking on the thirtieth?"

"Eight o'clock," she said.

"I have to get going," he said. "The train is here."

"Okay," she said. "I hope you had a merry Christmas yesterday."

"We did," he said.

She nodded, though he couldn't see her. "I love you, son."

"Love you too, Mom." He stayed on the line for just another moment, then he cleared his throat and ended the call.

Jennifer pressed her eyes closed and clasped her phone as she palmed it against her heartbeat. She faced the golden rays of light, the brightness of it painting the backs of her eyelids with pure whiteness.

"Thank you," she breathed into the breeze. Stu still might not come. His wife might not be so keen to forgive her. But he'd picked up his phone, and he'd said he loved her. Small steps, but steps nonetheless.

"How's the writing coming?" Jennifer glanced at Blanche's notebook as she passed her to her seat on the other side of the table. "This is a great location. How'd you get so lucky?" She pulled out her chair and sank into it. She'd been wearing her bathing suit all day, and today, it was a bright green and white one, done in a tropical leaf pattern. Her cover-up matched it, as did her white sandals.

She'd lifted her sunglasses when she'd left her balcony and entered the hallway, but she still wore her wide-brimmed beach hat. Also white, of course.

Blanche looked up from her paper, her pen still positioned just-so. She'd been hunched over it, almost like if she curved her shoulders the way she had been, no one would be able to see what she'd written.

But her handwriting was big and loopy and easy to read, so Jennifer could actually see it from here. Blanche caught her looking, and she straightened her shoulders and snapped the notebook closed.

"Good," she said. "I'm just catching up on my journaling."

Jennifer nodded, because Blanche had been keeping a journal since she was ten years old. She'd told Jennifer in college that the only way she ever got all the emotions out was through ink and paper. The only way she could make sense of the things that happened to her daily—big, small, or medium—was through writing them down.

"Do you still go back and read your journals?" she asked as a waiter approached. She looked up at him. "I want a carbonated lemonade, please."

"Hard Mike's? Or seltzer with wedges?"

"Seltzer with wedges," Jennifer said. She never drank while dealing with money.

"Another coconut cream?" He looked at Blanche, and Jennifer did too. Her eyebrows went up even as her smile curled her lips.

"Yes, please." Blanche smiled him away and lifted her empty glass to her lips. "You should try this. It's incredible."

"Are you writing jokes while drinking?"

"No." Blanche met her eyes. "It's virgin. No rum."

"Oh, so no fun then." Jennifer grinned at her. "And you weren't writing jokes anyway."

Blanche set down her pen. "Nope. And yes, I still go back and read my journals. I have several I'm working through right now, from when the girls were younger."

Jennifer nodded, trying to decide if she'd do that. "Why do you do it?"

Blanche sighed and looked over the railing. She'd been seated in the shaded section of the café, a coveted spot that always seemed to be full. "Right now, it's because my daughters are driving me insane. I want to see and be reminded of how much I love them." She returned her attention to Jennifer. "It's good to remember the busyness of life and know that even though dinner got burned and Greg was late coming home from work, we were together. We were a family."

"You're still a family," Jennifer said quietly, so much of what Blanche reflected on missing in Jennifer's own life. She'd told no one of her call with Stu that morning.

Not Mitch, when they'd met for brunch. Not Robin via text. For now, Jennifer needed to hold it close to her heart.

Love you too, Mom.

"I know," Blanche said. "But they think they know better than me now, so I like reading about the day April got her first pair of ballet slippers, and I was the one who knew how to sew on the ribbons." She smiled, drained the last few drops of cream from her glass, and set it down. "Now, you were going to give me some budgeting tips."

Jennifer laughed and shook her head. "No way. Not budgeting tips."

"You said you could help me with money."

"To stop spending it," Jennifer said. "Not setting a budget."

"I think I need a budget," Blanche said, once again looking away. She went away in those moments too, seeing and thinking about something not here at the table with them. "I've been thinking about it, and I think that would help me. Gregory always put me on a budget." Her lips trembled as she smiled. "Without him..."

She shook her head, and Jennifer knew the many and varied ways to finish that sentence.

"All right," Jennifer said. "I can help you with a budget if that's what you want."

"Really?" Blanche held such hope in her voice.

"Really." Jennifer picked up her phone from the

table and started tapping. "I use an app for on-the-go things. I have a much bigger system on my computer." To her credit, she'd only checked her financials three times in the past eleven days, a fact she was very proud of.

She tilted her phone toward Blanche. "It's called Evergreen. You can put your grocery purchases in it by scanning your store receipt. Gas works the same. You can set up your bills and then tap them as you pay them. Really, it's so I don't spend too much on coffee."

"And wine," Blanche said with a knowing look.

Jennifer blinked at her, shocked for a moment, before she started to laugh. "Fine. And wine."

Blanche giggled with her; their drinks arrived; and Jennifer started to squeeze her lemon wedges into the fizzy water. "Oh, you should've come with me to the Emerald Museum." She gave a happy sigh and sat back in her seat. "With your money, you'd have been able to afford one of the rings."

Her eyes sparkled like blue emeralds, and Jennifer couldn't help feeding off her energy. "I heard Frank was on the same excursion."

Blanche's smile vanished. "My dear brother is gossiping, is he?"

"Maybe." Jennifer finished with the lemons and stirred her drink. "Was Frank there?"

"Yes," Blanche said. "But it's not like you and Mitch. We're friends. That's all."

Jennifer held up one had. "All right. I believe you." She tapped a few times on her phone and said, "I just sent you an invite to Evergreen. And I have some sheets I can send you to fill out so we can establish your budget."

She picked up her phone. "I just need an email for that."

Blanche gave it to her, and then she said, "Okay, so how can I help you? Do you want to come to my room and watch the Ship Shopping Channel?"

Jennifer found herself blinking again, more rapidly this time. "There's a Ship Shopping Channel?"

Blanche didn't even crack a smile as she said, "Of course. How else would you be able to sleep at home if you didn't have the three-thousand-thread-count sheets that are on your bed here?"

Jennifer only hesitated for a moment before she burst out laughing. She had no doubt Blanche wasn't kidding, but she also couldn't see herself buying anything from the Ship Shopping Channel.

"Basically, you need to make a list of the things you like," Blanche said. "And buy a lot of them."

"Throw pillows," Jennifer said immediately.

"How many do you own?" Blanche took a sip of her drink, smacking her lips together.

"I don't know. A dozen?"

"Oh, honey, that's nowhere near enough," Blanche said. "Your job is to buy another dozen today. Online. Then make a list of things you'd like to buy. I can go over it with you."

"What if I don't want to buy anything?"

"Then why do you want me to help you spend money?"

"I just need to see that things will be okay if I do spend some money," Jennifer said, riddling out the sentence as she spoke it.

"Then go buy some towels from the Ship Shopping Channel, and you'll see that you'll be fine."

The purchases Jennifer wanted to make were bigger than towels or pillows, but she supposed she could start small and work up to paying for Duke's fishing boat. She'd already offered to do so, however, though Robin hadn't brought it up again.

"Okay," she said. "Now, tell me more about the old walled city you saw yesterday. Mitch said you have some spectacular pictures."

Blanche's face lit up, and she said, "I do," as she scrambled to pick up her own phone. Jennifer sipped her drink and looked at all of Blanche's pictures depicting the centuries-old town that had built a wall to defend against pirates and foreign invasions from the sea.

"It almost looks like France," Jennifer said, admiring the quaint streets with colorful façades and greenery hanging above the doorways. "Blanche." She turned the phone back to her friend. "Look how happy you look."

Her friend had a picture of her in front of a corner coffee shop with a bright blue door and the street fading into the background behind her.

"I do look happy, don't I?" Blanche smiled at herself

and then looked up to Jennifer. Nothing was said, but Jennifer knew the inner turmoil boiling in Blanche.

"It's okay." She reached over and covered Blanche's hand. "You can be happy and miss him at the same time."

Blanche nodded, and together this time, they looked over the water, nothing more to say.

Chapter Thirteen

Jennifer let her hand swing with Mitch's as they walked down the streets of Grand Cayman. They'd disembarked a couple of hours ago and had just finished breakfast at the cutest outdoor bistro.

"So I heard the best food here on the island is at this place called Chicken Chicken."

Jennifer looked over to him. "That's the name of the restaurant?"

His blue eyes shone with mischief. "Yep."

"Are you kidding?"

He chuckled and said, "I swear I'm not."

"I can't always tell with you." Jennifer wasn't sure why, but that bothered her. In general, she wasn't a big trickster. She disliked practical jokes, as she didn't think making someone else feel stupid was funny.

"I just think it's a funny name," he said. "And I think we should go later today, after we've snorkeled off all the calories we just ate and we're famished for chicken... chicken." He laughed at his own lame joke.

"You should leave the one-liners to your sister." Jennifer grinned with him, bumping him with her hip as they approached another jewelry shop. They'd already passed a couple, and of course, this one had someone standing outside of it too.

"Come inside," the man said. "We've got beautiful settings for you. A necklace? A ring?"

Jennifer opened her mouth to tell him they weren't interested, but Mitch said, "Come on, hon. Let's see if they have any engagement rings here that we like."

Her mouth dropped open, and he was able to tug her inside. Her legs had gone wooden, and she half-stumbled after him. Engagement rings?

Jennifer had never envisioned herself getting married again. She'd only recently started dating, but the pool of candidates on Five Island Cove wasn't big, to say the least. She knew everyone, and they knew her, and nothing had ever gelled or sparked.

Mitch followed the man over to a case, and he peered inside it as if seriously considering his options. Jennifer couldn't tell if this was another of his jokes or not. Surely it had to be.

"What do you like?" he asked in a quiet voice.

The salesman started detailing all they had, pulling out rows and rows of rings. Jennifer was getting blinded on every side, and she finally looked at Mitch. "You want to get married again?"

"I've thought about it," he said casually. Something flickered across his face, but he shuttered it away quickly, before she could truly identify it. "Oh, look at this one." He picked up an enormous diamond and showed it to her, clearly hamming it up.

The only way for her to get through this was to wade in, so she tried on a few rings, and then, much to the salesman's displeasure, they left the shop ringless.

Jennifer walked several paces with him, the tension between them new and unwelcome. "I've not seriously considered getting married again," she finally said. The words lodged in her throat after she said them, and she wasn't sure why.

"Why not?" Mitch asked. "Connor died a long time ago. You were only fifty-six, right? Plenty of time to find someone and get remarried."

She shook her head, her memories flowing fast now. "You remember what it's like to lose that relationship, right?"

Mitch's wife hadn't died, and his divorce was coming up on three years in a couple of months. "Yes," he said quietly. "You're not ready right away, I remember that."

"So then I'm sixty," she said. "And I'm buried in things I love. The cove is small." She lifted her free shoulder into a shrug. "I don't know. It never seemed like something I'd do. Or even be possible for me to do."

If there was one thing she'd learned on this cruise, it was that impossible things were possible.

"Then you came on a singles cruise," he teased, the

mood lifting. "What did you think was going to happen?"

"I have no idea," she said honestly. "You can't tell me you seriously thought your soulmate would be in a pool of one hundred, on a singles cruise. Out of the millions of people in the world. Billions, even."

Mitch laughed, the rich sound rising into the sky and making it bluer and better. "I honestly didn't know either," he said. "I came to get Blanche out of the house." He sobered and shot her a semi-nervous look out of the corner of his eye. "Honestly, I needed to get out of the house too. Retirement has not been good for me."

She nodded, because he'd shared that with her previously. "I came so I wouldn't have to be alone at Christmas," she said. "And it was one of the only things left. Did you know they book out those big cruises two years in advance?" She shook her head as he laughed again. "I think I got the last spot on this cruise, and I had to pay for the biggest, most expensive suite to do it."

"But it's the nicest," he said.

"It is." They continued down the street, but they didn't go in any more of the touristy shops. Another few blocks away, the stores turned more normal as the locals used them, and Mitch took her into a snorkel shop. She'd wanted to snorkel this whole trip, and the time to do so had finally arrived.

They rented the flippers and the goggles, as well as a couple of floaties, and then Mitch called a cab. "Cemetery Beach," he said as they got in, and Jennifer balanced her beach bag on her lap as Mitch piled their equipment between them.

The beach boasted white sand, as did all the beaches here on Grand Cayman. Cemetery Beach sat at the top of Seven Mile Beach, and Mitch's prediction that not many of their fellow yacht travelers would be there proved to be true. There wasn't another ship in port today, and the beach reminded Jennifer of the slower end-of-summer season on Five Island Cove.

After school had started and the local moms had retreated back to their homes. After the vacationers who'd come to the cove had to return to their regular lives and routines. Jennifer loved going to the beaches then, though the ones she was used to were definitely rockier than this one.

The beach filled her soul with life, and she sighed as she walked toward the water while Mitch filled their floaties with air. She wanted to dive right into the ocean and see the wonders it held beneath the surface. In her life, she'd learned that there was always something worth exploring beneath the surface of every person and every situation.

Hidden treasures. Sometimes some dangerous things, some things to watch out for. But people always had more to them than she'd originally thought, and she'd learned to give them the benefit of the doubt.

How she hadn't done that for her own children, she'd never understand.

"You've got to stop beating yourself up," she whispered, glad the wind here on the beach caught her words and flung them away. "It's time to move forward. You've apologized. You're going to sit down with them. Let this go."

Saying the words didn't magically make doing them easier. Or easy at all.

"Jennifer," Mitch called, and she took one last big breath as she gazed at the teal water, dancing in front of her. She turned back to him, crossed the sand, and stepped into him.

"Thank you." She pressed her mouth to his, glad when he easily wrapped her in his arms and kissed her back.

"What's this for?" he murmured against her lips. "I'm not complaining, mind you."

"Thanks for blowing up the floaties," she said. "Thanks for helping me free my mind on this cruise. Thanks for listening to me go on and on *and on* about my kids."

He swayed with her, and Jennifer let her eyes drift closed. There had only been a handful of people on the beach when they'd arrived, and no one new had arrived. She didn't normally kiss so passionately in public, but she didn't think anyone had seen them. Or would care if they did.

"Oh, you haven't gone on and on," Mitch said. "Besides, I get it. Adult children can be hard. It's not like there's a manual."

"I'm trying," she said.

"And a month ago, in their eyes, you weren't," he said. "You're doing great. Hey." He put one hand on the back of her neck. "Look at me."

She opened her eyes to do what he'd demanded. Kindness swam in his gaze. "You're an amazing woman, Jennifer. We all make mistakes. I think it's great that you're still learning, and you're willing to try to fix the things you've done wrong."

She didn't need his praise, but she could admit to herself that it was nice to hear. Her eyes burned, so she let her eyelids fall closed again. "Thank you," she murmured again.

He pressed a chaste kiss to her lips and backed up. "All right," he said. "We only have a few hours here before we have to head back for chicken and then get back on the yacht."

The rustling of a bag met her ears, and Jennifer got busy spraying sunscreen on her shoulders and arms.

"Look what I got." He held up something boxy, his face glowing. "It's an underwater camera."

Jennifer felt yet another gate in her life opening. "You're kidding."

"Nope." He grinned as he opened the box. "We get thirty-six shots, and I can't wait to see how they turn out."

"You have to get that developed?" She took the camera from him. "Do places even do that anymore?"

"There's an old shop in Jersey that does," he said.

"We have to wait until we get back to see these pictures?"

Mitch grinned harder, if that were possible. "Remember when you used to go on vacation and take pictures? You never knew what you'd see until you got back and developed the film. It's retro."

"Retro." She shook her head at his boyish enthusiasm. "All right. But...I don't live in Jersey. How am I going to see these pictures?"

He looked at her, only a slight particle of his joy subsiding. "Well, someone will have to go visit you, I suppose."

Jennifer shook her head, enjoying this game. She stepped into his chest again. "I don't like how you keep calling it a visit. I'm not your elderly mother in a long-term care facility."

He burst out laughing, but Jennifer was being dead serious. He laughed and laughed, only quieting when she handed him the can of sunscreen and turned her back on him. He sprayed the bare skin she couldn't reach, his warm hand rubbing it in nice and good.

She faced him again, and Mitch had sobered. "What would you like me to say? I'm going to see my beautiful girlfriend in Five Island Cove?"

"*See* is better than *visit*," she said. She put her hands on his shoulders as he brought them chest to chest. "Who would you be telling anyway?'

"My kids, for one," he said. "They've already been pestering me with questions."

"What kind of questions?"

"If I've met someone," he said. "Ella—my only girl—insists I must've, because I haven't been texting them on this trip." He rolled his eyes. "I've texted them plenty."

Jennifer thought the woman must have some reason, though. "Maybe not your usual things."

"That's what she said." Mitch grinned. "It's fine. I didn't confirm or deny, which only got my sons speculating too." He chuckled. "I'll be lucky if they don't send the Coast Guard to check up on me, honestly."

He bent and gathered the flippers. "Grab those masks and let's do this." He left his flip flops behind on the sand, and Jennifer hurried to grab the masks and follow him. She clumsily put on the flippers and donned the goggles and mask.

Mitch said, "He said you go out backward." He walked out forward until it got hard to do in the water, and then he turned around and added, "You just sit down into the water."

Jennifer was glad he demonstrated and went first, because she didn't know what that meant. He didn't sit down into anything that would support his body weight, but somehow he managed not to drown.

She followed him, turning around sooner than him as the water pulled against the flippers on her feet. She adjusted her mask, turned to face the beach again, and said a prayer. "Here goes nothing."

She sat too, and nope. Nothing caught her. She flopped like a hooked fish, her arms flapping to try to keep her afloat. Once she managed to find an equilibrium, her adrenaline rode up near her scalp.

Pushing herself out with the toes of her feet, she kept going until she couldn't reach the ground any longer. Only then did she admit this might have been a huge mistake. Her arms fluttered now, turning her toward the wider ocean. She couldn't see Mitch; she couldn't see anyone or anything. Just miles and miles and miles of water.

The sound of the sea echoed back to her, calming her, and Jennifer put the breathing tube in her mouth and pushed herself into a horizontal position. She immediately popped back up, because it was *not* natural to be able to breathe underwater.

She'd never done this before, and she needed a lesson. Irritation fired through her at Mitch's obvious abandonment, and she adjusted the tube again. Her mask dripped with water, and she put her face back in.

She exhaled out until she had almost no air left in her lungs. Then she drew in a long breath, and shockingly, it came through the tube without issue. She didn't try to swim or move. She simply needed to figure out how to breathe with her head in the water.

A few breaths later, she felt like she might be able to keep going. She kicked her feet up behind her and her body floated along the surface of the water. She kept her face down, her eyes searching the sand along the bottom of the ocean.

In that moment, a stingray swam beneath her, almost

adhered to the sand. She made a guttural sound as she yelped, and she lifted her head out of the water. "Mitch," she gasped, the tube falling out of her mouth.

He'd poked his head up too. "A stingray," she said.

"There's a school of yellow and black fish over here," he said, and they both went back to looking at the gorgeous display beneath the surface. Jennifer admired the stingray, though he'd gotten quite far from her in only a few seconds.

She followed Mitch several yards to a glorious school of black and yellow fish, hundreds of them swooping and swimming around one another.

She swam right into the middle of them, hoping with everything she had that Mitch was taking pictures. Such a new experience deserved to be captured for all eternity, and another buckle fell from Jennifer's inner defenses.

Maybe if she simply kept wading through life, she'd be able to find her way to the type of happy family life she wanted.

No, she thought as she continued on, following a bright blue fish that sure looked completely flat. *That's not how this worked. You didn't just wade in.*

She'd waded part of the way. Then she'd turned her back on the biggest, scariest thing in the world: the ocean. She'd dropped into it, flailed, gasped, panicked.

Then, she'd found her equilibrium. She'd practiced breathing. She'd become comfortable.

Only then had she been able to enjoy the beauty

living underwater. Only then had she been able to experience something she'd never experienced before.

So while her nerves continued to buzz at her about the upcoming arrival in New York—and who would be waiting for her to disembark—Jennifer would keep on swimming toward the goal she'd set for herself.

Chapter Fourteen

"Yes," Blanche said. "That was the final show." She sat heavily on her bed and reached for her makeup remover wipes. She'd had to ask Nahvi for them specifically, as well as some makeup, because Blanche certainly hadn't planned to perform her act for five nights on this cruise.

"Did you love it?" Eden asked. "Uncle Mitch made it sound like you're still a rock star on stage."

"I am," Blanche said, disliking that her daughter thought differently. "It's like riding a bike, you know?" She also didn't want too bright of a spotlight on her. Her daughters had grown up with a traveling, famous mother. For several years there, her face was on billboards in New York City, and she couldn't go anywhere without getting recognized.

That fame had faded. Other comedians had risen to her place. She'd receded quietly back to suburban life in

Jersey, and she hadn't hated it. The life she'd lived for the first fifty-five years of her life had given her these last ten with Gregory.

An extreme wave of missing hit her, and Blanche actually gasped.

"What?" Eden asked.

Blanche couldn't answer for a moment, her only focus breathing.

"Mom?" Ruth asked. "Are you still there?"

"Yes," she said, getting control of herself. "Sorry, I was just..." She didn't want to cover up her feelings anymore. Being on stage had reminded her that she was a person all her own. She, Blanche Gibb-Hanson, had value besides "Gregory Hanson's wife." She still had life to live, and she *should* live it.

"I was just missing your dad," she finally said. "He would've loved to see me perform again." She smiled just thinking about her biggest champion. He'd made it possible for her to travel by being home with the girls. He'd always supported her, and he'd always been the first person she tried out a new joke with.

"Mom," Eden said, a hint of chastisement in her voice.

"What?" Blanche asked. "I'm not going to hide it anymore, Eden. I'm allowed to miss him."

"Of course you are," Ruth said. "Eden, don't lecture her."

This was new, and Blanche stayed out of the sisterly bickering, which only went on for a few seconds. "Anyway," she said loudly. "I'll be home in a couple of days. We're stopping in Miami tonight. They bring on a couple of local shows and bands for our entertainment, and then we cruise all night and the next day back to New York."

"Are you glad you went?" Eden asked.

Blanche nodded as she let her feelings rise up and make themselves known. "You know what? I am. I ran in to Jennifer, and that's been amazing to get to know her again. I've made friends. I've been able to see that life is still good."

That alone had been groundbreaking for her. "Now, girls, I want all of us to get together when I get back. I have a few things to tell you." Just the thought of opening Gregory's office and showing them the mass of things she'd accumulated over the past nine months made her sick. But it had to be done. She needed to heal, and the only way to do that was to rip off the bandage.

"April should be back by New Year's Eve," Eden said. "Maybe we could have a party at the house, like we used to..."

"Sure," Blanche said, stunning both of her daughters into silence. She'd denied their suggestions for dinners, parties, and get-togethers at the house since Gregory's death. She hadn't been up to it, or she didn't want to deal with so many people in her house.

Now, she couldn't wait to hug her daughters and her sons-in-law, pick up her grandchildren and kiss them, and tell everyone about the amazing things she'd seen and done on this cruise.

She stepped into the bathroom as Eden started detailing how Blanche wouldn't have to do anything. She'd bring all the food. Ruth would decorate.

Blanche looked at herself in the mirror and started wiping the makeup from her face. She recognized the blue eyes looking back at her. Sure, she'd gotten older in recent years, but the young woman she'd once been still lived inside her.

She was a completely new person than who she'd been when she'd boarded this yacht. Blanche had more confidence now. She could own how she felt instead of trying to bury it behind purchases—though she had gotten a set of the bath towels from the Ship Shopping Channel. That was out of *necessity*, though, not boredom or the attempt to control something in her life.

She looked the same on the outside, but she felt washed out and brand-new on the inside.

"Mom," Eden said. "Really?"

"Yes." Blanche turned away from the mirror. "Let's have the biggest New Year's party ever. We could all use it." She wanted to face the New Year with hope, and now that she'd emerged from this cruise a new woman, she saw no reason to cling to the past nine months of pain and misery.

"I have my special credit card in the jar on top of the fridge. Remember that?"

"Yes," Eden said slowly. "You want me to use it?"

"I'm not going to be able to plan a party," Blanche said. "You only have five days, so get out the credit card and get good food."

A moment of silence passed between Blanche and two of her daughters, and then the three of them started to laugh. Blanche hadn't had a good, long, cleansing laugh in a long time, and hearing her daughters join her only added more joy to that filling her from the toes up.

THE YACHT ALWAYS SEEMED TO MOVE. IT CUT A confident path through the water, the captain knowing exactly where they were on the globe, though Blanche could only see blue in every direction.

It rocked to and fro, even tied to the dock, and Blanche didn't like being on the boat while it was in port. She'd much rather disembark and find something new and excited to do or eat.

Unfortunately, their next stop was Miami, a city she'd visited many times. She remembered a good strip of restaurants along the water, and her mouth watered for a good Cuban sandwich.

She stood at the railing, the yacht getting closer and closer to the men waiting on the dock. They'd be here tonight, with entertainment just down the waterfront, and part of Blanche didn't want to go. She craved the non-moving ground beneath her feet, her known and familiar recliner, and her TV playing quietly while she wrote in her journal.

In short, she wanted to go home and stay there for a while. The need to leave where she stood rose within her, just the way it had as this trip had approached. She'd been eager for the cruise, if only to prove to Mitch how wrong he was about her.

Turned out, he hadn't been wrong. Blanche listened to the sound of the sea as the water rushing past the hull of the yacht lessened, quieting. But now new waves lapped against the yacht, creating more slapping and splashing sounds than the rushing sound of water.

She tried to hear the hidden messages the ocean whispered to her, but she hadn't been able to fully harness its language. With only two more days before this vacation ended, Blanche wasn't sure she'd ever be able to understand what the sea was trying to tell her.

"That's what you're wearing?"

She rolled her eyes as Jennifer came to her side. She wore a glittering, gold dress that probably had a thousand sequins on it. Blanche herself had worn plenty of designer outfits over the years, but she'd steadfastly refused to wear shiny things from head to toe, as well as turtlenecks.

Tonight, she'd put on a party skirt that barely brushed her knees. Sure, it was navy blue, not exactly "party material," but good enough for a seventy-year-old woman. Her blouse screamed tropical, as she'd bought it in LA at the Silver Sails gift shop while she and Mitch had waited to board the yacht.

Bright pink, blue, and green flowers covered the sheer white fabric, and she'd put a tank underneath to preserve her modesty. Jennifer, on the other hand, seemed to be taking "party appropriate" to a new level.

"Yes," Blanche said. "This is what I'm wearing. You're planning to go clubbing?"

Jennifer flashed a brief smile and said nothing, something she'd been doing all day today. Blanche had always been able to read people, and the moment she and Mitch had returned from their snorkeling adventures in Grand Cayman, Jennifer had been more distant.

"You don't have to tell me," Blanche said. "But I know something's bothering you."

"Perhaps," Jennifer said. A sigh leaked from her mouth, and she turned toward Blanche and leaned her hip into the railing. "You know what? Yes. Something is bothering me." She'd just gotten fired up, and Blanche faced her too.

"What is it? Something my dear brother said?"

Jennifer's eyes narrowed. "No, it's my kids," she said. "And kind of something he said about them."

Blanche didn't want to know, so she held up her hand. "I know you and Mitch are new," she said. "There's no way you can know everything about him after only two weeks."

"I sense a but," Jennifer said.

"Not a 'but,'" Blanche said. "Just...he's a man,

Jennifer. He wants to have a relationship with his kids, but it was Courtney who maintained a lot of that for him. Since their divorce..." Blanche shrugged and moved away from the railing as the boat started sliding sideways into the dock. Ropes got thrown and voices shouted as the men on-board worked with those on the dock to secure the vessel.

"Since the divorce, my ex-wife has enjoyed more visits from my kids than I have," Mitch said.

Blanche spun to face her brother. "That's all I was going to say."

Mitch's blue eyes blazed like the hottest part of a fire. He glanced over to Jennifer, who again stayed silent. "What are you two talking about?"

Blanche could not be in the middle of this. She held up both hands, noting Mitch's freshly pressed black slacks and his sharp button-up in a shade of blue that only the Caribbean Sea could achieve.

"Not my place," she said. "I'm sorry I brought it up."

"I brought it up," Jennifer said. "Because I'm tired of suppressing everything and dealing with it never." She gave Blanche a smile and leaned in to hug her. "You look wonderful. Maybe give us a few minutes, and we'll come find you?"

"No problem," Blanche said. She cut a look over to Mitch, and her brother nodded. That was Blanche's cue to leave, and she did so as quickly as possible. With any luck, she could get off the boat and skirt over to Little

Havana for a taste of the Cuban food she currently craved before Jennifer and Mitch finished their little chat.

As she stepped onto dry land, a sense of relief filled her. At the same time, she swore she heard a whisper in her head saying, *Come back, Blanche. The water's fine.*

She turned to face the water again, the last of the daylight fading into twilight. She did love the ocean, and she would be back soon enough.

"Blanche," a man said, and she turned around again to find Frank standing with a couple of other people. Four, maybe five, actually. They all looked her way. "We're headed to Little Havana for a bite to eat before the concert. Do you want to come?" He looked back to the yacht too. "Or are you hanging out with Mitch and Jennifer?"

Blanche didn't have to think twice. She could send a text and be fine. "I'd love to come," she said, hitching her smile in place. After all, he was going the same direction as her, and she might as well enjoy some company one last time before she sequestered herself back into her quiet house in the New Jersey suburbs.

Chapter Fifteen

"I didn't know about your children," Jennifer said as she and Mitch wandered away from the line of people waiting to leave the yacht. Normally, they'd be in it, but she needed a quiet place to talk to him for a few minutes first.

"I wouldn't expect you to," he said. They reached the bow of the boat, and no one stood there. "I didn't mean to upset you."

She knew that, which was why she hadn't said anything earlier today. She nodded now and looked away. "It's not really that big of a deal. I'm just tired of bottling things up like they don't matter."

Mitch simply stood near her. "What did I say?"

Jennifer's first instinct was to wave away his question, deal with this ping in her chest on her own. She'd done it plenty of times in the past. She stopped herself, because her feelings were valid too.

"I know you don't know the entire situation with my kids," she said. "But I didn't like how you dismissed my fears that they wouldn't be waiting for me in New York."

"I apologize."

She nodded again, her gaze still skirting past him for some reason. "I want you there too." Jennifer finally faced him and ran her hands up his chest to his shoulders. He likewise put his hands on her waist, and just like that, they stood in one another's arms. "But Mitch, I *need* my kids there. I've known for months now that I need to do something about my relationships with them, and you dismissed it, like having you there would be enough."

He nodded. "I'm sorry."

"Thank you." She touched her lips to his, barely making contact before pulling back. "I don't want you to be upset with me." She whispered now, her heartbeat almost louder than her voice. "But I don't want them to meet you in New York. They don't even know it was a singles cruise, and I want to save the conversation about us for another time."

She barely dared to look up at him, but when she did, she found kindness and acceptance in his eyes. "All right, Jennifer," he murmured. "Whatever you want."

"So tomorrow night," she said. "We'll have our farewell dinner. Just the two of us. On my balcony. I checked with Juan Carlos, and he said he can bring plated dinners to my room. I just have to request them twenty-four hours in advance."

Mitch's smile appeared, his larger-than-life approach to things shining through. "Did you schedule those already for tomorrow night?"

"Yes, sir," she whispered. "Six o'clock." She played with his collar. "I'd love to see you in another shirt like this. I have another fancy dress I can wear."

"Sounds amazing," Mitch said.

Jennifer nodded and stepped out of the circle of his arms. "Come on. We don't want to leave Blanche alone for too long."

"She's different," Mitch said as he took Jennifer's hand in his. "My sister. This cruise has been good for her."

"I feel different too," Jennifer said, smiling at the ground as she took her first steps back toward the disembarking zone. "It's amazing what some fresh sea air will do." She glanced over to him, glad to see him smiling. "I'm sorry about your kids."

Mitch's grin faltered. "I suppose I have a lot of work to do with them," he said. "The same as you. It's been hard on all of us—this divorce."

Jennifer nodded. She'd never been through a divorce, so she had no experience to speak of. "Especially you," she said, half-guessing.

"It hasn't been easy," he admitted. "I'm past my ex-wife, to be clear. But I feel...useless. I don't have my job anymore. The kids are grown and relying on Court. She doesn't need me. It's like...what am I doing with my day? My time? All this money I've saved up?" He shook his head. "Sometimes it feels really pointless, don't you think?"

"Sometimes," she admitted. "Which is why I want to have better—more authentic—relationships."

"Does that include me?" he asked.

"Yes," she said without a moment of hesitation. They joined the line to leave the boat, which had shrunk considerably. "I'm not hiding you. I just want New York to be about my kids." If Stu would come. She'd been praying for him to find a way to soften his heart enough to be in the city when she got off the yacht. She couldn't keep begging for the same things over and over, so her pleas had switched to herself.

Petitions to the Lord that *she* would be able to handle whatever happened two mornings from now. That *she* would have the strength she needed if Stu didn't come, or if Robin couldn't make it. She was essentially asking her daughter to pay for an airplane ticket to greet her as she got off a cruise ship.

Mitch held up his phone. "Blanche ditched us."

"What?" Jennifer grabbed his phone and read his sister's text.

Gone to Little Havana for a bite to eat before the concert. Catch up to you there.

"Gone to Little Havana." Jennifer scoffed. "Sure. This has Frank Bellasi written all over it." She searched the dock below, then the street beyond, but she couldn't see Blanche.

Mitch chuckled, though Jennifer didn't see anything

funny about the situation. "What?" she asked. "You're the one who spent fifteen minutes raving and pacing in my room when you caught them in the elevator together."

He shook his head, his smile still too wide for Jennifer's liking. "I trust Blanche," he said. "And I wouldn't want her wandering down to Little Havana alone at night anyway."

They left the yacht, and Jennifer was content to hold Mitch's hand and let him decide where to go and what to do. He asked, "Do you want to try a restaurant, or do you want to go to the Silver Sails reception at the concert venue?"

He looked left, toward downtown Miami. And then right, toward South Beach, where their nightly entertainment would be. The cruise line had also set up a buffet for passengers, so they didn't need to wander the city in search of food.

Jennifer looked left too. "I'm thinking something non-cruise line." She'd been eating that food for two weeks, and Miami was sure to have an eclectic range of culinary choices.

"Downtown it is," Mitch said, and they stepped off the curb together.

THE FOLLOWING EVENING, JENNIFER RUSHED into her bathroom to put in her second earring. For whatever reason, she hadn't been able to do it by feel, and she needed the assistance of the mirror. She'd barely slid the hook through the hole in her earlobe when a knock sounded on her door.

Three light raps, and that would be Mitch. She couldn't just yell "Come in!" and then hurry to slip into her heels while he waited in the living room. She exited the bathroom, stepped into the sleek, shiny, black heels, smoothed down her dress and her wig, and went to answer the door.

Mitch stood in the hallway, wearing a pale yellow shirt and a tie that matched his navy slacks. "Well, well," she said. "It seems like someone might be lost."

He grinned at her and scanned her from her auburn wig that boasted curls halfway down her back. Her lips were practically nude, as this wig did all the talking for her.

"Wow." Mitch openly stared at her. "I think I am lost. I thought this was cabin three-twenty-five." He looked at the door. "Sure seems like it is, but I don't know who this gorgeous redhead is."

He entered her suite anyway, taking her into his arms and kissing her despite the fact that the door still stood wide open. He slid his hands up her sides to her face, where he held her while he continued to kiss her.

After several long seconds, he pulled away. Jennifer leaned into him, all of her strength gone with a simple kiss. Because, truth be told, it was not a simple kiss. It had said a lot of things, and Jennifer needed to take a page from Blanche's habits and write down everything she'd just learned about Mitch Gibb and his feelings for her.

Without the time, she simply opened her eyes and smiled at him like she'd had too much to drink. "The food should be here any minute." She let the door swing closed as he stepped past her with a murmur of acknowledgement.

Tonight wasn't about food, and both of them knew it. Jennifer figured she might as well address the elephant in the room and get it over with. Or rather, the elephant now out on the balcony.

She followed Mitch outside, the wind definitely more biting now that they were churning up the Atlantic Seaboard toward New York City. She shivered and said, "Maybe I should've had them set this up indoors. I forgot we're not in the Caribbean anymore."

"I'm sure they will," Mitch said. "Do you want me to move the table right now?"

She wasn't even sure it would fit through the door, but she nodded. The doorbell rang to her suite, and she hurried back toward it to answer it. Juan Carlos and two assistants smiled their way into the room, the last one pushing a silver cart with covered plates on it.

"Sir, we can do that," he said, and he and one of his assistants set about getting the table into position in her room instead of outside.

Nerves ran through her for some reason, but Jennifer managed to stay out of the way and stay quiet. Once the food was placed and Juan Carlos had bowed his way out of the room, Mitch pulled out a chair for Jennifer.

She sat, giving him a warm smile as she did. He did too, then unfolded his napkin and lay it on his lap.

"This isn't the end for us," she blurted out. "You know that, right?"

He looked at her, his eyes somewhat guarded. "Yes," he said carefully, the way she'd expect a prosecutor who didn't want to give away his whole hand quite yet would.

"It's goodbye for a very short time. You have my number; I have yours. I'm asking for one day with my family, and then you can call and text me all you want." She picked up her fork and removed the cloche still hiding her food. "Come to the cove every weekend. I don't care."

She met his eye, desperate for him to understand why she didn't want any distractions tomorrow. Mitch reached over and covered her hand. "Jennifer, I can't come *every* weekend." He cracked a smile, and Jennifer almost threw her napkin at him.

Instead, she lifted her chin high and spread her own napkin across her lap. "Of course not," she said with plenty of diplomacy in her voice. "I know how to get to New Jersey too."

That sunk into the silence in the room, and the delicious beef short rib on her plate didn't have enough power to distract her from the man beside her that she'd been getting to know, kissing, and starting to fall for.

"How'd you know I've been worried about us?" he asked.

"Because you kissed me like it was the last time," she said. "I didn't like it. I mean, I liked it. But I didn't at the same time."

"Not the last time," he murmured as he skated his fingers up her forearm. "Should I try again?"

She grinned at him and leaned toward him. "You better."

He kissed her again, and this time, it didn't feel like he was trying to get every last taste he could before something amazing disappeared. He kissed her slowly, with passion, until she felt like someone had finally seen her for who she was, and they hadn't run screaming.

No. In fact, Mitch *liked* who she was, and he wanted to keep getting to know her, and he'd give her tomorrow with her kids, but not one minute more.

Chapter Sixteen

Jennifer tugged her shawl tighter and wrung her hands, wishing she'd thought to bring a pair of gloves. She'd known she'd be ending the cruise in New York City, and that it was nearly New Year's. Not exactly tropical in this neck of the woods. Not exactly quiet and serene either.

Part of her wanted her to jump over the side of the yacht. They were close enough to land now, surely, that she wouldn't drown. In fact, the shoreline sat only a couple hundred yards off her balcony.

The sane, rational part of her knew she hadn't been swimming in several years. Wading into a gently lapping ocean wasn't near the same thing as pitching overboard into chilly water and stroking toward the sand.

The sand wasn't even close to the tropical, white sands on Grand Cayman, which Jennifer thought was her favorite spot she'd seen on the cruise. Going through the Panama Canal had been her favorite experience, and she swallowed hard at the idea of doing something like that with her children and grandchildren.

"As long as we all have our own space to relax," she murmured. The sound of her voice got blown away by the airhorn on a much bigger ship. Jennifer startled and looked over her shoulder, but of course, only the wall of her suite looked back at her. The ship must be on the other side of the yacht.

Jennifer retreated to her room quickly, thinking perhaps the much smaller yacht was about to be plowed under by a bigger boat. No such thing happened, of course, and she set about making sure her already-packed bags were packed.

She wore the wig closest to her regular hair already this morning, and if the clock embedded in the wall could be trusted, she had less than twenty minutes to be ready to disembark.

She'd said good-bye to both Blanche and Mitch last night, but now, she wanted to see them both again one last time.

The only thing she hadn't tucked into her tote yet was her charging cable for her phone, and she unplugged the device and lifted it at the same time. She quickly dialed Mitch, because perhaps he could come first, she could steal comfort from him one last time, and then they could text Blanche.

Surely he'd be helping his sister prepare to leave the yacht, and as his line rang so did her doorbell. She turned toward it, expecting it to be a staff member from Silver Sails, as she'd opted to have them remove her luggage from the vessel.

Sure enough, a sharply dressed young man stood there, a professional smile on his face. Someone's phone rang in the corridor, and Jennifer hastened to end her call before Mitch's voicemail picked up.

"Sorry, ma'am," he said. "I just need your bag." He peeled off part of a sticker and handed her the claim tag with the backing still on. The other piece got stuck to the top of her bag, and he smiled again as he towed it out of the room.

She caught sight of another gentleman waiting in the hall behind the luggage trolley, and her heart leapt against the back of her tongue. Mitch.

They waited while the attendant loaded her luggage onto the trolley and left, and then Mitch raised his phone. "You called?" he asked with that handsome grin.

"I'm so nervous," she admitted. Jennifer didn't like this feeling in her stomach. The way the bees swooped and swarmed and made her feel like she might throw up at any moment. She wasn't used to it. Since Connor's death, she'd taken the reins of his investments and businesses, and people got nervous around her, not the other way around.

This is important, she told herself, and a vein of humility ran through her. Yes, she needed to humble herself. She couldn't march from this yacht with her wigged head held high as if the world should bow at her feet.

She had to admit her mistake out loud to her children and grandchildren. It couldn't be avoided, and as Mitch wrapped her in his strong arms, Jennifer didn't *want* to avoid it. She had the distinct feeling it would only make her stronger.

"One last kiss," she murmured. "For strength."

"And I'll call you tonight," he said. "Late, like nine."

She nodded, and then he lowered his mouth to hers. Jennifer took what she needed from him, and then she gave back as much as she could. Several seconds later, he pulled back. She said nothing, because her throat had gone so, so narrow, but Mitch said, "You've got this."

AN HOUR LATER, JENNIFER FINALLY STEPPED onto New York City soil. Fine, concrete. Asphalt if she was being technical. She had to continue down this walkway and inside to the terminal, and then she'd be able to be reunited with her loved ones...if they'd come.

She hadn't been able to bear the thought of texting to ask if Stu and Robin were waiting for her. If she got a *no* from either of them, Jennifer felt certain she'd burst into tears, and she'd rather do that in private.

She wasn't sure if she should steel herself for disappointment or hope for the best, and the two feelings warred inside her with every step.

Her chest buzzed with wasps, and no amount of deep breathing could calm them. In fact, all that did was make her light-headed. She entered through the automatic sliding doors, her vision blurred from the lack of oxygen and her heart positively pounding in her chest. It beat so hard, surely her ribs would break.

Noise assaulted her inside, as did a rush of blessed heat. There seemed to be another group of people gearing up to embark on their cruise, and Jennifer scanned the sea of faces, trying to find a familiar one.

"Mom!" a woman called, and she turned to her left. Not someone she knew. Would there be someone she knew here?

Please, she prayed. *Surely Robin would've come.*

In front of her, a man she recognized from the yacht moved to his right, and then Jennifer came face-to-face with none other than Anna-Maria.

She wasn't exactly the person Jennifer wanted to see, but she practically ran to her and sagged into her daughter-in-law. "You came," she sighed into Anna-Maria's shoulder.

"Stu's dealing with Gene," Anna-Maria said. She pulled away from Jennifer, and their eyes met. There wasn't a sudden understanding between them, but pure vulnerability streamed through Jennifer.

Anna-Maria moved to the side and looked over her shoulder, and Robin stood there. Duke stood with both girls, and Jennifer let herself start to cry. Robin and Duke engulfed her in a hug together, and Jennifer couldn't help the sobbing that started.

It wasn't instant forgiveness, but they'd come. Jennifer didn't realize until that moment how much she'd doubted that they'd even be here.

"You're all here," she said through her tears. Her voice sounded like it belonged to someone else. "You didn't all have to come."

"We wanted to, Grandma," Mandie said, cutting a glance to her mother. They shared the type of close relationship Jennifer wanted to have with her daughter but hadn't been able to build. She wasn't even sure why she'd spent the past fifteen years building walls instead of relationships, and she didn't know how to tear them down.

One piece at a time, she supposed. One conversation at a time. One experience at a time.

"Hey, Grandma." Jamie stepped into her, and Jennifer held her tightly against her chest.

"How are you, my darling?"

"She's right there," her son's voice said, and Jennifer stepped back from Jamie. She didn't immediately rush to her son, because Robin had often accused her of preferring him and his family over hers.

That wasn't true, but Robin lived in the cove. She saw her daughter and her family far more often than Stu's and Anna-Maria's. So when she could see them and spend time with them, it sort of turned into an event.

Stuart stood with his wife now, both of their boys with them. Jennifer did not see Eva anywhere.

With all the busyness around them, Jennifer marveled that her attention could be laser-focused to such a small space. Only a few people. "Hello, Stuart," she said as she moved toward him. "Thank you so much for coming."

He received her into his arms, and Jennifer pressed her eyes closed and committed this moment to memory. She couldn't remember all of the angry words that had been spoken the last time she and Stu had been in the same physical space. They didn't matter any more.

"I'm sorry," she whispered into her son's ear. "I really am."

He said nothing, and when Jennifer backed out of his arms, he wore a storm of indecision on his face. He looked to his wife, who frowned at him. Anna-Maria had some hot Latina blood in her veins, and she'd never held much back. At least that Jennifer knew about.

Watching the two of them have their silent argument was more than Jennifer could handle, so she drew her grandsons into her for a hug too. "How are you Gene? Your mom said something was wrong?"

"I just nicked my finger on the pole there." He held up his hand, which didn't bear a bandage, but did have a tiny cut on the side of his pointer finger.

"He shouldn't have been touching it," Henry said, ever the older brother.

"Shut up, Henry."

"Both of you knock it off," Anna-Maria said. "Or I'll

put you on the subway home, and we'll go to breakfast without you."

Jennifer's heart grew a tiny pair of wings. "Did you guys have time for breakfast? They don't give us breakfast on the ship."

"At all?" Gene asked.

"Our meals were mostly lunches and dinners." She smiled at her youngest grandchild and drew Jamie into her side too. "Us old folks aren't up early enough for breakfast. Coffee is all we need."

Jamie grinned at her, and Jennifer marveled at how tall she'd gotten. "Have you grown a foot since I left the cove?" She smiled at her granddaughter, who shook her head.

"Well." Duke clapped his hands together, the sound far too loud for Jennifer's liking. Normally, she would've given him a disapproving glare and moved on with the conversation. Now, she simply looked at him, waiting for more. "I didn't give up a day of fishing to stand in a ship terminal. Mandie's told us about an amazing place here in Brooklyn, and Anna-Maria confirmed it's the best place for breakfast."

He nodded toward the door. "Should we?"

"What about your luggage, Mom?" Robin asked, and Jennifer stopped in her tracks. Her luggage.

"Oh, uh, let me see if someone can hold it." She glanced around the terminal, but the number of people inside seemed to have doubled.

"Mom, let's get it and take it with us," Stu said. "It's

not that far to No Yolk, and they'll let us keep it at the table." He met Duke's eyes, and the two men nodded. "We have a reservation we don't want to miss. Nine people is a lot for a small city restaurant."

Jennifer's desperation flared. "I don't know how to get my bag." She turned in a full circle again, and this time Robin stepped to her side.

"Mom, let's go over here where it says 'Luggage Retrieval.'" She looked at her husband. "Take everyone else outside. We don't need to stand in here."

"You heard your mother," Duke said. "Come on, ladies. Outside."

Robin led her mother over to the luggage retrieval area, and Jennifer saw several people from her yacht. This must be the right place. She saw her bag and yelped. "It's right there."

A man wearing the same uniform as those from Silver Sails onboard the ship pulled the bag and set it in the same row as several others. Jennifer found her confidence again and went to retrieve it.

She lifted the handle and turned back to Robin, coming face-to-face with Mitch. A smile moved through her whole body, and she gave him only a shy part of it.

"Good luck," he whispered as she went by him.

"Talk soon," she said back, and then she rejoined her daughter and left the building, only to be blasted with the iciest wind she'd ever felt.

"My goodness." She tugged the shawl higher over her exposed neck and throat, but even that wasn't enough for this New York winter. “I forgot I’d be coming home to these conditions.”

“You don’t have a heavier coat?” Robin asked. She positioned her earmuffs over her ears and pulled a pair of gloves from her coat pocket.

“No.” Jennifer had her shawl and that was all. She hadn’t been planning to spend any time in the city, and she eyed the line of people waiting with their luggage for a cab. That would’ve been her, had she not asked her kids to meet her for breakfast.

She painted a smile on her face and found the rest of her family waiting down the sidewalk a ways. “I’ll be fine,” she said. “Let’s go.”

Stu took one look at her as she approached, sighed, and pulled out his phone. “I’m calling for a ride.”

“It’s fine,” she said in a haughty voice. “Just because I’ve been on a boat for a couple of weeks doesn’t mean I can’t walk.” She smiled fondly at Henry, and the fifteen-year-old smiled back.

“Mom, it’s thirty degrees.” Stu rolled his eyes and kept tapping. “Four minutes.”

Jennifer wondered if she’d make it for those four minutes, or if she’d freeze to death first. Her teeth chattered slightly, but she pressed them together to make them stop.

She looked at Mandie, who’d bundled in a dark gray hat with a snowy white tuft on top of it. She wore laughter in her eyes, and she let it out of her mouth a moment later. "Grandma's freezing," she said amidst the giggles. "Look how hard she's trying not to show it."

"My word." Robin pulled her earmuffs off and put them on Jennifer, who dodged.

"I'm fine," she said.

"Your ears are bright pink," Robin shot back as she managed to get the earmuffs over Jennifer's ears. "Wear these. I have a hood." She flipped it up and snuggled down into it—as well as into Duke's side. Even he had a thick black coat, gloves, and a hat. He unwound his scarf and put it around Jennifer's neck.

She hadn't always been the nicest to him, but he adored her daughter, and Jennifer had always given him credit for that.

"Thank you," she murmured.

"Sure," Robin said as Duke nodded. "She'll take it from *you* without arguing."

Jennifer looked at her daughter, noting the sourness there. Usually, she'd snip back at Robin. The situation would become twice as tense. This time, Jennifer smiled and took her daughter's gloved hand. "Thank you for letting me use these. I might not die in the next two minutes."

Robin softened, and Jennifer felt one brick in one of her walls crack and turn to dust.

She wasn't sure if standing on a sidewalk outside a cruise terminal in Brooklyn was the best place to tell her kids the biggest truth they needed to hear. The words rose inside her anyway, threatening to spill everywhere, in any order.

"Robin," she said. "Stuart."

They both looked at her, and she found her courage in her daughter's eyes. She'd told Robin a little bit about the money already. She just needed to keep talking.

"I have over sixteen million dollars in cash, investments, property, and other financial assets. I spend a great deal of time managing them, and I'd love to start showing both of you—or one of you—what I do, so you're not blindsided the way I was when your father died."

Robin blinked, faster and faster she blinked.

"Mom." Stu didn't say anything more. He worked in real estate here in the city, and he did quite well for himself.

"Duke." Jennifer turned to him and lifted her freezing fingers to his bearded face. "Thank you for loving Robin so completely. I should've done this years ago, but I was too proud. I'm so sorry, and I hope you can forgive me for that."

"Jennifer, you're fine," he murmured.

She lowered her hand back to her side, having nothing else to do with it. "Nevertheless, I'd like to pay for *The Soaring Eagle*. All of her. Down to the last cent. You and Robin work so hard. *So hard*. I know it. I *see* it, though I've never it said to you."

Tears filled her eyes. "I'm sorry I've never said it." Her face froze as the tears slid down her cheeks. She quickly wiped them away, but more followed. "I'm very proud of both of you—and your girls—and I want to pay for the boat."

Duke's mouth fished, though surely Robin had told him that Jennifer had offered this already. Over the phone, over a week ago.

She turned to Stuart. "I cannot believe I let my tongue get the better of me. I love you and Anna-Maria and your children, and I did not mean to pass judgment on Eva, or you two as parents."

"Thank you," Anna-Maria said swiftly, before her husband could say anything. She glared at her husband, continuing that silent argument from earlier. "Your son knows this. He's just...grappling with a few things right now."

Stu looked away, so Jennifer couldn't decipher the unrest in her son's expression. He cleared his throat, but said nothing.

"I'd like to pay for the apartment."

"No way," Stu said instantly, and even Anna-Maria's eyes grew wide.

"It's got to be almost the same amount as a fishing boat." She flicked a glance to Robin. "I want it to be fair. Equal. Fifty-fifty. There are no favorites here."

Robin ducked her head then, and Jennifer thought she might have seen the hint of tears in her daughter's glassy eyes before she did.

"So." She drew in a deep breath. "I can show you two together, or separately. Robin is older, Stu, and typically, that's who you put in charge of your estate once you die."

"Mom," Robin said. "You're not going to die."

"You never know when you'll go," Jennifer said. "I learned that when your father died." She shook her head, allowing the sadness that came, even after all these years. "He was very young, and I've done the best I could with his money."

She looked at both of her children. "Truth be told, I let it consume me. I let it rob me of being a real person, because it doesn't make sense to give out huge gifts to my adult children. At least...I'm working on it making sense. I'm trying to think of it as *helping* my children, whom I love and want to have in my life, more than *giving* it to very capable and very strong adults."

Her smile wavered on her face. "I fear the money and managing it has made me cold and callused. Only interested in doing something if there's something in it for me." Tears splashed her face again, and Jennifer fisted her fingers instead of wiping them away. "I don't want to be like that anymore."

"Okay, Mom." Stu stepped into her and wrapped his arms around her. "Okay. It's okay." He held her for several seconds—until a car pulled up to the curb.

"Stuart?" a man called, and Jennifer stepped back. Duke put his arm around her, gave her a steadying smile, and waited while Stu confirmed they were the party to be driven to the restaurant.

"Thank you, Duke," she murmured again.

"See?" Anna-Maria said to Stu as they herded their children toward the sedan. A mini-van pulled up behind them. "Aren't you glad I made you come now?"

"That minivan is for us too," Stu said without answering his wife. Jennifer was still trying to figure out what she'd said. "We'll go in this car. You guys can fit in there?"

"Yep," Robin said. She went down the sidewalk with her girls, and Duke and Jennifer followed.

She paused at Stu's side. "You didn't want to come?" She wasn't attacking him, but she wanted the whole truth out there.

"It was hard for me to come," he admitted. "We couldn't get Eva to be here."

"Oh, don't you dare," Anna-Maria said, spinning back from the sedan she'd been about to sink into. "Our daughter won't even talk to him," she spat, mostly at him, but partially at Jennifer too. "He has plenty to apologize for too, and I'm thrilled I *forced* him to be here today, so he can see that it's okay to humble yourself, swallow your pride, and ask for forgiveness."

"Anna," Stu said in a very tired voice. He reached up and wiped one hand down his face before looking at her with pure exhaustion in his eyes.

"For all the crap you talk about your mother, at least she's finally doing the right thing." Anna-Maria looked at Jennifer, her strong emotion still splayed across her face. "Thank you for your apologies. They mean a lot to me, personally, and to Stuart, though he might have trouble expressing it. *I* will be sure to communicate them to Eva, and if you'd text her and keep trying to talk to her, I think she'll come around."

"Of course," Jennifer said as diplomatically as she could. She hadn't meant to get Stu in trouble with his wife.

Anna-Maria glared at Stu one last time, then returned to the sedan.

"Come on," Duke said quietly. "Let's hope this minivan can drive fast, or we're going to miss our reservation."

Chapter Seventeen

Blanche exited her bedroom, expecting to enter the kitchen of her New Jersey home to all three of her daughters. Only two sat at the small dining room table in the eat-in kitchen, and her little poodle trotted along at her side.

"Morning," she said to them before focusing on her teapot. Eden and Ruth much preferred coffee, and Eden, in all of her uptown snobbery, had brought her specialty blend. She could only get it at one grinder down on Market Street, and it was all she would drink.

She'd been trying to convert the rest of them to this "outstanding" blend for years, but the only time any of them drank it was when she made it for them.

"Mom." Ruth got to her feet instantly. "Look at the cupcakes." She squealed as she practically threw her phone at Blanche.

Irritation bolted through her, and Blanche worked

to tamp it down while she looked at the adorable cupcakes on her daughter's device. "Those are amazing," she said, handing the phone back. "When can you pick them up?"

"Right now," she said. "Once I have them, I'm going to swing by and get the rest of the catering from Joseph's. April's coming with me, and Eden's going to stay here and decorate. Right, Edie?"

"Right," Eden said, the first word she'd spoken that morning. She seemed ultra-focused on something on her phone, and that was fine with Blanche. Out of her three daughters, Eden was definitely the loudest. The one who talked and talked and talked. The one who had to process things verbally instead of internally.

Blanche had gotten used to it over the years, but that didn't mean it didn't wear her to bone sometimes.

Not right now, she told herself. Her girls would all be here for their big New Year's Eve bash, and Eden had bought a new type of candy to try every hour, on the hour, from six p.m. to midnight.

She was planning to blow up balloons and put activities in seven of them, one for each hour from six to midnight. Blanche had told her several times she wasn't sure if she'd make it past ten, but Eden had said that was fine; she could go to bed at any time.

Blanche had not told them about the office full of things she'd bought. She needed to, and soon, because her small, three bedroom, two bathroom house couldn't hold its secrets for much longer. They'd had enough room to raise the girls here, with a modest piece of land and a flat driveway for riding bicycles.

Once they'd grown up and moved out, Gregory had converted one of the bedrooms into an office, while Blanche had kept the other made up and ready as a guest room. Both Eden and Ruth, along with their husbands and children, lived within an hour of Blanche, and they rarely needed a bedroom to sleep in.

April had gotten married and moved to the Midwest, so when she and her family came to town, they sometimes used that bedroom. They had three children now, one of whom had just turned twelve, and a single guest room no longer sufficed.

For this trip, April and Noah had rented a house not far from here on one of those vacation rental sites. They'd be here through the second, when they had to get back and get ready for school to start again.

Blanche busied herself with making tea, and Ruth went back to the table with Eden. Both of them tapped, tapped, tapped on their phones, and Blanche didn't mind. She loved the silence, and the familiarity of her own home, and having her girls here.

The front door opened about the time Blanche's tea kettle sang, and she quickly flipped the gas off to silence it as April walked in. "I'm here," she said, and Blanche thought of Jennifer's story about her husband getting home every evening at six and calling that he'd arrived.

They'd exchanged a few texts last night, and Jennifer had said things had gone well with her kids. They were going to meet together in a few weeks, and Jennifer would go over the financials with them.

It felt strange to Blanche that she needed to do the exact same thing, but something entirely different too. Eden had asked about money, but she hadn't been concerned. She didn't need to be, because Blanche had enjoyed a near-celebrity career and all the dollars that brought with it. Gregory had been employed well too, as a city manager in a neighboring metropolis.

"Good," Ruth said. "Let's go." She got to her feet again.

"I just got here." April bypassed her sister and moved into the kitchen. "Hey, Momma."

"Hello, dear." Blanche smiled at her youngest and hugged her. Her heartbeat began to quiver in her veins. She pulled away from April and poured the hot water over her tea bag with shaking hands.

"Are you okay?" April asked.

Blanche looked up and found April watching her hands. Her eyes came up in the next moment too, concern riding there plainly. "Mom."

"This has to steep for a few minutes," Blanche said. "Girls." She cleared her throat. "Can you—can we all put our phones down for ten minutes? I have to show you something."

Ruth had already stood, and she placed her phone on the counter. April did too, as this was something she and Gregory had done with their girls several times over the years.

"Eden," she said. No answer.

"Eden," Ruth barked.

Eden finally looked up, her eyes glazed. "What?"

"Mom needs a phone-free moment," Ruth said. She rolled her eyes as she turned away from her sister. Blanche wanted to tell her to be more patient with her. Ruth was an excellent middle child, but she also wanted to prove she was better than Eden sometimes. Even now, as an adult, Blanche caught her doing it.

She wouldn't like getting a lecture either, so Blanche held her tongue. "Ten minutes," she said. "If that. Then you can go do your pick-ups, and Eden can get decorating." She smiled, though ever cell in her body trembled. "And where are the kids? The husbands?"

"Mine are sleeping in and doing a lazy breakfast this morning," April said.

"Dan will be here in about twenty minutes with the kids," Eden said, finally placing her phone in the row with the other two. "They're bringing all the décor."

"Noah's working today," Ruth said. "He's got the youngest two with him, and Shannie is babysitting for a neighbor. They'll be here tonight."

Blanche nodded, because while she hadn't hosted a party like this—or even attended one—in a while, a new, quiet excitement built inside her. She couldn't think of anything better than being surrounded by her children and grandchildren. It was the perfect way to ring in the New Year.

"Then I'll have time to walk Misty before I come

help with the decorations." She smiled at Eden, who returned the gesture, plenty of questions in her eyes.

Blanche took a deep breath and looked at April. "Will you go open your father's office, please?"

April's expression grew panicked, and even Eden gasped. "Mom," she said. "You haven't been in there since he died."

"Actually." Blanche followed April down the hall that branched off the kitchen and living room. "I have. I've been lying to you. I've been..." Well, they'd see.

April reached the door and looked back to the three of them. Eden and Ruth pressed in close behind her. "Lying to us?" Ruth whispered. "Mom, what do you mean?"

"I've been in his office," she said simply. She nodded to April, and her youngest twisted the knob and let the door settle open. She looked inside, her eyes widening and widening.

"Momma." She was the only one who ever called Blanche "Momma," and her kids called Blanche "Grandmomma." She loved the differences, glad their East Coast family had been touched by the Midwest.

"What is it?" Eden pushed past Blanche and stepped in front of April. She sucked in a tight breath and entered the office without another word.

April followed her, but Blanche stayed in the hall. Ruth linked her arm through Blanche's, and she looked at her daughter. Ruth looked the most like Blanche, with plenty of thick, blonde hair. She didn't color a single strand of it, and it looked almost muddy these days.

Blanche smiled at her. "It's not that bad."

"Eden's always been a bit of a drama queen." Ruth smiled, though it looked scared on her face. "He's not in there, is he, Mom?"

"You think I have your father's dead body in his office?" Blanche scoffed, then started to laugh. "You watch too many crime documentaries."

"Perhaps," her daughter said.

"Mom." Eden appeared in the hall with four pairs of shoes in her arms. "What are you going to do with four pairs of Gimiks?"

"They pull on easy," Blanche said, remembering the early-morning segment on the shopping channel where she'd learned about these shoes. "They're perfect for old folks like me, who can't bend over to tie their shoes." She made a half-hearted attempt to swipe the shoes from her daughter.

Eden made an exaggerated sway away from her, her blue eyes firing with lightning. "Four pairs, Mom?"

"Most of this stuff hasn't even been opened," April said from within the office.

Ruth exchanged a look with Blanche, and then she too, headed into the office. Blanche did not follow. Still quaking, she returned to the kitchen and stirred her tea. She added honey and moved to sit at the table. The four of them could fit, and she waited for her daughters to return to her.

One by one, they did, Eden arriving last. She sat at the head of the table, her arms folded.

"It's called grief spending," Blanche said quietly. "Comfort shopping. Retail therapy.." She studied the amber color of her tea, stirring it to make the surface ripple. "It makes me feel...in control of something again."

"Do you even have the money for this stuff?" Eden demanded.

"Eden," Ruth said. "My word."

"Mom was a famous comedienne," April said. "She has plenty of money." A pause filled the kitchen. "Right, Mom?"

Blanche finally looked up. She surveyed the worried —and yes, angry—looks on her daughter's faces. "Everyone grieves in different ways. I know each of you has had to go through a terrible tide of things in the past few years. I wish I could've been a better support for you in the past nine months, but I barely felt like I was keeping my head above water."

A wicked smile curved Eden's mouth. "You could probably use that inflatable pool in there to help you."

"Eden," April and Ruth both chastised at the same time, but Blanche started to laugh. And laugh, and laugh, and laugh.

"Probably," she said amidst the giggles. She got up and moved to Eden's side. She crouched down and let her daughter put her arm around her. "I love you, Eden. You're a master at organizing things." She looked up at her strong, somewhat brash daughter. "Will you help me go through it all and have a yard sale?"

Eden's nose wrinkled as she frowned. "In the winter?"

Blanche ignored her and turned to Ruth. "I'm getting control of it. Do you think you and Noah could help me finalize a budget? I started one with a friend of mine on the cruise, but you could really help me take it to the next level."

Ruth's eyes glowed. She'd been an accountant for a few years before she'd gotten married and started having babies. She did bookkeeping for a few clients now, but she wasn't actively trying to grow her business or take on anything new.

"Of course I will, Mom."

Blanche nodded and looked to April, who raised her eyebrows. "Was this friend on the cruise a man or a woman?"

Blanche's knees ached in their position, and she groaned as she straightened. Back in her seat, she lifted her teacup to her lips for her first sip of chamomile. The silence in the house could've choked a man.

"It was a woman," she finally said. "My old college roommate, in fact."

"No way," Eden said.

"That's great," April added.

"She's very good with money, whereas I am not. We... helped each other, actually." She smiled at the remembered conversations she'd had with Jennifer. "She lives out on Five Island Cove—and, here's the best part." She hit the T's hard on the last two words. "Are you ready for this?"

"I sense something juicy." Eden's face glowed now, and her arms had unclenched.

"She and Uncle Mitch hit it off. Started dating and kissing." Blanche made a face. "It was all very...singles cruise."

"Uncle Mitch!" April squealed and started laughing.

"Oh, I can't wait to ask him about her," Ruth said with glee. "When will he be here?"

Blanche grinned and grinned at her girls. "He said about mid-afternoon. He's going to make his 'famous chili dip' for our smorgasbord of food tonight."

The laughter died away, and into the new, easy silence, Eden said, "Uncle Mitch has a girlfriend. Wow. Who knew someone as stuffy as him could loosen up enough to charm a lady?"

That got them all laughing again, Blanche included. She didn't tell her daughters that their uncle wasn't *always* the stuffy lawyer he had to be for his job. They'd had a picture of him in their mind, and it wasn't anything like the casual, easy-going, quick-to-laugh man wearing tropical swim trucks aboard a luxury yacht.

"We have to go," Ruth said. "Come on, April." They got up, gathered their phones, and left to go pick up the catering they'd ordered. As they went out the front door, Eden's husband and children came in. Laden with bags and boxes of party supplies, all of them entered the kitchen and started putting things down on any available surface.

Blanche smiled at her grandchildren, gave them hugs and kisses, and told them there was a bag of cookies in her bedroom. The two of them scrambled off to get the treats, and Blanche rose to hug Dan.

"Thank you," she murmured to him.

"I hope this doesn't overwhelm you," he said. "You just escape if you need to."

"What would overwhelm me?"

"This is the biggest piñata they had?" Eden practically screeched the statement, like she couldn't believe such a tiny piñata could exist.

Blanche and Dan turned toward her, where she stood holding an absolutely enormous Chinese lantern, done in red and gold and black tissue paper. It was easily three feet tall and two wide, and Blanche had no idea where they'd even hang that thing.

"My goodness." She covered her pulse with her palm. "That's huge."

Eden continued to frown at it, and then she set it down. "It'll have to do."

"*That* could overwhelm you," Dan muttered, and Blanche couldn't help giggling. Eden could be overwhelming just by herself. Arm her with a piñata...and all bets were off.

Blanche wanted to be here for this, though, and she sent a quick text to her brother. *I told the girls about your fling aboard* Sweet Sea Dreams. *They were shocked that a "stuffy lawyer" could get a lady on a singles cruise. Maybe wear that toucan shirt you bought in Grand Cayman and show them a different side of you?*

She added a couple of laughing emojis and sent the text before tucking her phone away. After all, she didn't need to be buried on a device when so many good people and things were happening in 3D, right before her eyes.

"FIVE, FOUR, THREE, TWO, ONE! HAP-PY NEW Year!" Blanche counted down and shouted with everyone else, her face aching from how much she'd smiled this evening.

Her girls had outdone themselves for this party, and tears rolled down her face as she stepped into Mitch's arms. "Thank you," she sobbed against his shoulder. "Thank you for making me take that cruise."

He said nothing, which was why the girls thought he was so stuffy. He hadn't dressed in anything tropical, and he hadn't defended himself about his relationship with Jennifer. His nieces had questioned him about it and her ruthlessly for the first half-hour after he'd arrived at the house, and he'd taken it all in stride.

That was how Blanche knew he really liked Jennifer. It wasn't a fling at all, something he'd mentioned to her as they'd loaded their plates with apricot-glazed kielbasa and then his special chili dip. She did love it with melted cheese and plenty of corn chips, and she swore she'd never have to eat again.

"Momma, don't cry." April took her from Mitch, and then Ruth piled into the hug, and finally Eden. Blanche wanted to open her arms wider, so they'd all be completely engulfed; safe under her mother's wings.

Of course, she couldn't do that. She'd had to clip them free years ago, push them out of the nest, and watch them fly. They'd all done spectacularly too, and Blanche's tears kept streaming as she whispered how much she loved them.

She drew in a deep breath, it being the first year in forty-one that she hadn't had Gregory at her side to welcome a new year to their home. Now, she had to do it alone. Now, she had to be a party of one. Now, she had to be the woman she'd always been—before him, with him, and now, after him.

"Happy New Year," she said in a much quieter voice. With her girls, her brother, her sons-in-law, and her grandchildren around her, Blanche felt confident in adding, "It's going to be a great year."

Chapter Eighteen

One month later

Jennifer knew today's brunch didn't have to be perfect. She still flitted around the island in her house, changing the angle of the butter dish, then nudging the jam jar to the side to make room for the utensils.

She'd bought new ones just for this occasion, and she couldn't believe how nervous she was. Not only that, but the gold-plated forks did nothing to ease the butterflies flapping in her chest.

The doorbell rang, and then Robin called, "We're here, Mom."

"Come in," Jennifer called back, finally placing the platter of candied, spicy, thick-slab bacon on the counter near the honeyed ham. She'd been cooking for two days for this, and she wiped her hands on her apron, then untied it as her daughter and Duke entered the back of the house.

"It smells amazing," Duke said. "Wow, look at this spread."

"Mom," Robin said. "You made too much. It's just us." Their eyes met, and Jennifer simply smiled. It wasn't just them today, but she hadn't told Robin that.

She hugged her and said, "Hello, dear," before stepping back. She folded her apron neatly and tucked it in the drawer next to the stove so she could find it the next time she wanted it. "Let's take care of the un-fun stuff first."

A quick removal of a magnet freed the check she'd written from the fridge, and she extended it toward Robin and Duke. They stood side-by-side, a power couple, united in all things. Including this.

After a moment, Duke took the check and looked at it. He whistled, the kind of sound that said, *Wow, this is a lot of dough.*

And Jennifer wouldn't even miss it.

"Put that away," she said. "It's done. Over." She pasted a smile on her face again. "Now, I have to tell you something."

"Thank you, Mom." Robin lunged at her and held her tightly. "I know we're still learning around each other. I know I've hurt you over the years too. I'm sorry for whatever I've done that has caused you grief."

"You have nothing to apologize for."

Robin sniffled, stepped back, and said, "Nothing you might know about." She exchanged a quick glance with Duke. "But we both have things to apologize for."

Duke nodded and held up the check he hadn't put away yet. "Yes, Jennifer. I'm sorry, but we really do appreciate this. So much." He too hugged her, and Jennifer loved clinging to a big, broad pair of shoulders.

She imagined Connor standing in front of her, not Duke, and she let herself miss him for a few powerful beats of time.

Duke cleared his throat and folded the check in half. It disappeared into his back pocket, and they faced one another. "You had something to tell us?"

Before she could say another word, the doorbell rang again. Her eyes flew in the direction of it, though she couldn't see around corners. "Yes," she said. "But I guess it'll be a surprise."

She flashed a quick smile, ignored Robin as she asked, "A surprise? What kind of surprise?" and went to answer the door.

Mitch stood there with a huge pitcher of bright pink liquid, his offering to this brunch. He called it "cherry cordial" though it wasn't the darker pinks she'd seen in any cordials she'd drunk before. He claimed it had a minimal amount of alcohol and he could serve it as a cocktail or neat.

At this moment in time, Jennifer simply wanted him to put it down and kiss her. Instead, she drank in his tall frame, his bright smile, and the way he chuckled infectiously.

Blanche stood at his side, and she carried something

much more practical—a platter of smashed, crispy, roasted potatoes.

"I left you a spot on the counter for those," she said, nodding to Blanche. "My daughter and her husband are already here." She stepped back, out of the doorway, and nodded down the hall. "Straight back."

Blanche entered first, pausing to give Jennifer a kiss on the cheek. The pair of them had flown in yesterday, and they'd all gone to dinner here in the cove. She'd orchestrated this brunch this morning, specifically to pay for the fishing boat—she'd needed to work out a few tax-related things with her bookkeepers and accountants—and to introduce Robin to Mitch.

She'd kept her last relationship a secret for a long time, and she wasn't willing to do that this time.

"Good morning, handsome," she said to him as he entered the house. She took the glass pitcher from him and set it on the credenza that stood guard near the door. "You're dangerous with this."

"You said you didn't have white carpet."

"I don't." She eased herself into his arms. "But you can't kiss me with that."

"I bet I could," he murmured as he lowered his mouth to hers. She wasn't going to make out with him in her foyer, with Blanche down the hall with her daughter. So she kissed him quickly, pouring as much passion as she could into a couple of strokes, then broke their connection.

She tucked her hand in his, picked up his cherry cordial, and faced the rest of the house.

Robin, Duke, and Blanche all stood at the end of the hall, only one of them smiling. "Guys," Jennifer said. "This is Mitchell Gibb. We met on the singles cruise and have been seeing each other since."

Duke grinned and reached out to shake Mitch's hand. "Good to meet you, fella."

"You too."

"That's Duke," Jennifer said. "My daughter's husband. Robin, my oldest." She beamed at her daughter, glad when Robin snapped herself together, blinked finally, and shook Mitch's hand too.

"And this is Blanche Gibb-Hanson, of the super-famous comediennes." She grinned at her new, old friend. "She was on the cruise too, and we were college roommates."

Robin pulled in a breath. "You're Blanche Gibb. My mother has told some great stories about you." She looked back and forth between Jennifer and Blanche.

"Was there one about a badger?" Blanche asked, a devilish glint in her eye.

"No," Jennifer said firmly, though her smile suggested Blanche could tell this horrifying story. "You're not telling that." She started to laugh, which only set Blanche off too.

"She has to tell it now," Mitch said. "Don't you think, Robin?"

"Absolutely." She smiled at Mitch. "You know, you don't seem like my mother's type."

That sucked the oxygen out of the room, and Jennifer cleared her throat of her last giggle. "What does that mean?"

"He's...charming." Robin grinned at him and cocked her head. "Fun. You have a light I can feel."

"He softens me," Jennifer said. "Is what you mean." She handed Blanche the cordial and stayed close to Mitch's side. In true Mitch fashion, he hadn't said anything.

"No." Robin's eyes flicked to Jennifer's. "You don't need to be softened, Mom. I think he complements you. He likes you how you are, and you let him be how he is. That's what two people who are so different do for one another." She leaned into Duke's side, and with his hand on her hip, she looked up at him. "Like us."

"Like us, baby." He kissed her, and it was true that Duke was more of a ruffian than Robin. He was a fisherman, with big, callused hands and a loud voice. Robin planned weddings and ran on the beach. They did complement one another, and as Jennifer looked at Mitch, she did soften right in front of him.

"Well," he said. "You said she was sharp."

Robin stopped kissing her husband and smiled at Mitch. "It's great to meet you. Come in, come in. What did you bring?" She stepped over to the island and let Mitch tell her about his cherry cordial.

Once that was done, Jennifer indicated the plates.

"Thank you so much for coming, everyone." She grinned around at all of them, and she couldn't stop. "I love you all so much." Only Mitch's eyebrows went up, and Jennifer could admit she didn't love-love him the way she needed to in order to marry him.

But on some level, she loved him. She loved him as a friend. As someone who did see her, flaws and all, and liked her anyway. They'd had some great conversations in the past month, and when she'd gone to Brooklyn last week to see Stu and give him his check, Mitch had come into the city as well.

They'd spent a fabulous weekend together, wandering Fifth Avenue and Central Park, eating in great restaurants, and continuing their relationship. Now, he was here. Blanche would leave tomorrow, but Mitch was planning to stay for another week.

He was retired, he said, and had nothing else to do.

"We can eat," Duke said. "But I really want to hear this badger story..."

Jennifer met Blanche's eye, and the two of them grinned in tandem. Blanche picked up a plate and put a piece of Jennifer's homemade raisin bread on it. "Okay, but you can't blame me if you never look at your mother-in-law the same way again."

I hope you enjoyed THE SOUND OF THE SEA! That something spoke to you, maybe in a language you can't quite understand, but can feel. **Please leave a review now! <3**

Read on for a sneak peek at **THE LIGHTHOUSE**, which is the first book in the Five Island Cove series. You'll get to see years of Jennifer's strained relationship with her daughter that leads up to this amazing, satisfying resolution. **Read now - the ebook is free on all retailers!**

Sneak Peek - The Lighthouse
Chapter 1

Robin Grover picked up the basket with the red-and-white checkered cloth, her tears filling her eyes and almost flowing down her face. She would not cry yet. As soon as she saw Kristen, she wouldn't be able to hold back the tide. But she still had a fifteen-minute drive and a five-minute hike before she could release the emotions.

"Ready," she said to herself, looking around the office where she ran events. The house sat empty during weekdays, with Duke off on his fishing boat until at least one or two in the afternoon. During peak fishing season, he didn't come home until the fish dried up, sometimes for days at a time. He'd been gone for a few days, and Robin expected to hear from him by evening.

The boxes on her planning table could wait. For once, the anniversaries, birthdays, and family reunions of the rich and famous could simply *wait*.

Joel Shields had died, and surely even heaven had paused for a moment to welcome him home with open arms.

His wife, Kristen, was still here, and Robin had quickly collected all of the woman's favorite things, tied them up in ribbons and cloths, as if that could erase the stunning pain of losing someone you loved.

Her emotions hitched again, and Robin laced them behind a brave smile and clenched her fingers around the handle of the basket. She moved, knowing that for her, doing something helped her tame the urge to scream and beg to know why. Yes, staying busy had often kept her mind off the more unpleasant things in life.

She made it behind the wheel of her minivan, and she managed to drive across Diamond Island on autopilot. She wasn't sure if the lights she went through were green or not, but she didn't get hit, so they must have been.

Kristen and Joel Shields had lived in and ran the lighthouse on Diamond Island, the largest of the five islands that made up Five Island Cove, for almost four decades. Located off the coast of Connecticut, north of Martha's Vineyard yet west of Nantucket, Five Island Cove was the epitome of a quaint New England life. South of Cape Cod, the islands were nestled right in the center of the triangle made from some of the most popular vacation destinations for the rich and famous. Once the celebrities and ultra-rich had discovered the islands, vacation homes, weekend getaways, and tourism had soared.

Robin had lived on Diamond Island for her entire life, and while she often thought she would've liked to have seen more of the world, she couldn't imagine living anywhere but on a mound of earth surrounded by water. She loved the sound of the waves as they washed ashore. She adored the way the sun glinted off the water. And once she'd married Duke Grover, she'd had all the lobster and soft-shell crab she could want.

Gratitude for the life she'd been given streamed through her, and Robin allowed a tiny trickle of tears to slip down her face. She sniffed and swiped them away as she pulled into the small parking lot at the lighthouse, somehow there already.

The water in front of her undulated as it usually did, and Robin watched it for a moment. The sun shone today, and it likely would for many more days to come, as they'd just come into spring and were well into April. The flowers had started to peek up from their winter naps, and Robin couldn't wait for the rose bushes along the edge of this parking lot to bloom.

Joel had planted all of them, each a different color, until a few years ago. He'd planted a pink lemonade variety for her, and Robin tensed from head to toe. She exhaled and rolled her neck, trying to get some of the tightness to go. She felt suffocated with grief, as if someone was leaning against her windpipe and she couldn't get enough air.

She found she couldn't quite get out of the vehicle, and she peered up at the lighthouse through her window.

She'd thrown an absolute bash the day Joel and Kristen had retired from their post here. Their son, Reuben, had taken over the job of making sure the glass was polished, the light beamed out into the darkness, and that ships and smaller craft navigated these waters safely.

Diamond Island was aptly named for its shape. It also sat at the head of the other island, with the cove they created on the opposite side from this lighthouse. This side contained more cliffs, more rocks, and more wind. Oh, the wind could steal a breath from a person before they could identify the thief.

The flag on top of the lighthouse didn't seem to be flapping too hard, but Robin could see Alice climbing the ladder one cold day in November to replace it. The job had to be done from time to time, and all of the Seafaring Girls had had to do it at some point.

A shaky smile touched Robin's mouth. Her friends in the Seafaring Girls had been Robin's lifeline. They'd been as close as sisters, sharing clothes, shoes, and stories for so many years. She'd slept at Alice's for a couple of weeks one summer when the fighting with her mother had become unbearable for both of them, and Alice had come to Robin's the moment the funeral had ended.

Alice had replaced the flag with great triumph, and the other girls had clapped and whooped for her. She'd been the bravest of them back then, and Robin wished she hadn't let so much time go by since talking to her.

Reuben lived in the lower two levels of the lighthouse

now, but Robin could still see herself knocking on that deep, navy blue door around the back of the lighthouse. Kristen would always answer, and words didn't even need to be said before Robin stepped inside. Sometimes she went alone, but usually, she came to the lighthouse with her sisterhood.

Memories of the four girls she'd been best friends with growing up streamed freely now, and she wondered if anyone had alerted them of Joel's death.

"Probably not," she said to herself, still looking at the clapboard white lighthouse. It looked like Reuben had painted it recently, though Robin knew he had not. She would've noticed such a chore, as it took scaffolding and time to get the entire lighthouse as gleaming as possible, and the job was done once a year.

She'd seen no scaffolding in her last few visits to Kristen and Joel, and come to think of it, she hadn't seen Reuben or his wife either.

The roof of the lighthouse was the same navy blue as the door around the back, and the whole structure stood tall and proud, right on the edge of the island. Robin remembered the first time she'd come here, and she'd felt like she could see clear across the ocean to another continent.

She couldn't, of course. But she'd felt both powerful and small in that moment, and then she'd met Alice Williams, also at the lighthouse for the first time. Then another girl came. And another. Kristen had led a sea adventure group for girls for years, and Robin couldn't even imagine how many lives she'd touched through the Seafaring Girls.

In that very moment, she once again felt both powerful and small. What had she done with her life? Had her time on earth meant anything, to anyone?

Her chest tightened, and she hated the feeling of teetering on the edge of a steep cliff, about to fall off. She'd felt like this when it had been her turn to replace the flag on the top of the lighthouse, like one misstep and she'd go tumbling down. The stakes back then had been steep, sure. But now, they felt astronomical, like if she didn't choose correctly, everything would shatter.

She drew a deep breath, reached for the basket, and got out of the car. Step one, and she'd done it.

When Reuben had taken over the lighthouse, Kristen and Joel had moved into the cottage up the hill a bit, and Robin glanced at the minivan parked as close to the path as a vehicle could get. She remembered the day she'd gone with Kristen to buy it. The day Joel hadn't been able to get into a vehicle that stood higher off the ground, but he also couldn't stoop down to get into a sedan.

Cancer was a cruel master, and Joel had suffered with it for five years before succumbing to its unrelenting grip.

She sniffled as she started up the path, keeping her eyes on the asphalt at her feet. Step two, get moving. Done.

"I was wondering when you were going to get out of that car."

Robin looked up to find Kristen standing on the

path, wearing a black sweat suit that seemed like it had been tailored just for her.

Their eyes met, and Robin wouldn't have been able to hold back the tears then, even if she'd wanted to. "Kristen," she said, her voice breaking. The woman was twenty-two years older than Robin, but age didn't matter right now.

"I should've known you'd be the first to come. Joel's been dead less than twenty-four hours." Kristen's smile shook on her mouth, and she looked out toward the ocean.

Robin stepped toward her, her vision blurry from the tears. "I'm so sorry. I won't stay. I just brought you a few comfort items." She reached Kristen and folded back the checkered cloth. "Those chewy Werther's you like so much. A new visor, because I thought you might like to sit on the upper deck and watch the waves." She glanced up at Kristen but didn't want to make eye contact. "And of course, cookies."

Always cookies. It had been the cookies that had first bonded the two women together, and Robin couldn't look at a cookie of any variety without thinking of Kristen.

She practically shoved the gifts at Kristen and then latched onto her, the embrace awkward with the basket between them. "I'm so sorry. I loved Joel so much." Her voice was little more than air and a squeak, but she didn't know how to make it sound normal.

There was no more normal without Joel.

Kristen moved the basket and hugged Robin properly, both of them crying. For some reason, when Kristen wept that validated Robin's feelings, and a sense of relief and belonging flowed through her.

A minute or two later, Kristen pulled back. "Okay." She wiped at her eyes. "Let's take this to the deck."

Robin nodded, clearing the water from her own eyes and face. She looped her hand through Kristen's arm as they turned and walked back toward the lighthouse. They went through the navy blue door and climbed up instead of down, emerging onto the upper deck and winding around to the side that faced the water.

A sigh moved through Robin's body, and she asked, "What do you need help with?"

"Nothing," Kristen said as she sat in one of the chairs on the deck. There were only two, and Robin had sat up here with Kristen countless times before. "Joel had everything planned, right down to the day the funeral should take place." A small, fond smile sat on her face as she looked at the waves. "He wanted it on a Saturday so people wouldn't have to take work off to come."

Robin nodded as she sat. She leaned forward, keeping her elbows on her knees. "I can go to the funeral home with you, Kristen. You shouldn't have to do that alone."

"Jean is here," Kristen said softly. "And Clara is trying to come."

"Oh, okay." Surprise moved through Robin, and she

couldn't help asking, "You want to go with Jean or Clara?"

Jean was Reuben's wife, and she'd thrown a literal fit about moving to Diamond Island and living in a lighthouse. She'd cried for a solid month after she'd arrived, and she'd gone to the doctor to get on anti-depressants after she'd gained thirty pounds in the first year they'd been here. She went back to Long Island where her parents lived for long stretches of time, and Robin would be surprised if Jean had the fortitude to go to the funeral home with her mother-in-law.

"No," Kristen said. "I don't want to go with either of them." She looked at Robin, and a quick snort came from her, followed by a laugh. "Jean didn't offer. And Clara's still trying to get a flight in."

Clara was Joel and Kristen's daughter, and she also lived off-island. Like a lot of people, she'd left Five Island Cove as soon as she could, and Robin hadn't seen her in years.

She wasn't sure what had driven Clara away. Robin loved the big, summer homes of the rich who only came in the warmest months. Robin participated—and sometimes planned—all the small-town traditions that made Five Island Cove the gem that it was.

Every island had its own charm and celebrations, and each was only a short ferry ride from the others. They created a crescent in the vast waters, with the cove coming ashore on the biggest of the islands, Diamond Island.

There was great seafood and other delicious restaurants, most of them family-owned for generations. The picturesque Main Street had picture-perfect shopping, which had only gotten better as people with more money helicoptered or sailed in for their retreats on the island. Why Clara hadn't liked that, she wasn't sure. People paid a *lot* of money to come to Five Island Cove, and yet some of the people who'd grown up here wanted to run from it.

"So I'll go with you," Robin said, smiling. She reached across the space between them and took Kristen's papery hand in hers. "And I was thinking..."

"Here we go," Kristen said, but she squeezed Robin's fingers. "You and that brain of yours."

Robin ducked her head, not quite brave enough to say what was on her mind while looking at Kristen. "I think I should call all the girls. Get them back here for the funeral."

Kristen's grip on Robin's hand increased, and then she let go. "They won't come."

Robin looked up at the pain in the older woman's voice. "Sure they will," she said. "You and Joel meant a lot to us."

"You might get Alice and Eloise," Kristen conceded. "But if you can get Kelli back here, you'll be lucky. And AJ? You'd have worked a miracle."

Robin had always liked a good challenge. At the very least, she'd never shied away from one. "Well, I guess it's time to work a miracle."

Sneak Peek - The Lighthouse Chapter 2

Eloise Hall reached for her phone as it rang, the last grades for the semester about to be finished. She just had one more class to go, and she'd be free until fall semester.

"Doctor Hall," she said.

"Eloise," a woman said.

A rush of memories filled Eloise's mind with that voice. Slightly high, always a bit on the self-important side, but with a foundation of kindness. "Robin?" Her heart started beating in a strange, syncopated way. She hadn't spoken to Robin—or anyone from Five Island Cove—in a long time. At least five years.

Too long, Eloise thought, as she had in the past. But she'd done nothing to bring the once-close group together. It was always Robin or Alice that did that, and Eloise shouldn't have been surprised to get a call like this out of the blue from the power blonde.

"Yes," Robin said. "How are you? Did you know you're very hard to get in touch with?"

"Am I?" Eloise sat back in her luxury office chair, her grading forgotten. She pictured Robin from their youth, the image of the pretty, perfect, perky blonde girl a very hard memory to get rid of. Funnily enough, Eloise had never been jealous of Robin, though she'd been very popular. AJ had always had the most boyfriends, but that was because she wasn't afraid to sneak off with the boys in the dark and do things Eloise hadn't done until college.

"Very hard," Robin said with a smile in her voice. "It's so good to hear your voice."

Eloise didn't know what to say, so she said nothing. She'd spent the last twenty-seven years in college, as a matter of fact, as she'd attended Boston University after leaving Sanctuary Island, one of the islands that made up Five Island Cove, gone on to get her doctorate at Harvard, and then returned to BU as a professor.

Biology she knew. How to have a conversation with someone she hadn't seen in years she did not. Her mind niggled at her that she did know Robin, almost as well as she knew her own self. Still, it felt like the five years stretched until a chasm existed between them, with Eloise on one side and Robin calling to her from the other.

"Anyway," Robin said, filling the silence. "I'm calling because Joel Shields passed away, and the funeral is next Saturday."

There was no invitation there, but Eloise heard it anyway. "Oh, no," she said, her past marching through her mind now. Damn Robin for opening that door. Eloise pressed against it from the other side, but it would not close all the way. "That's terrible news. I knew he was sick, but..." She let the words hang there, because while she'd gone to visit her aging mother a couple of years ago, she hadn't thought much about the Shields' since she'd heard the news of Joel's cancer.

"Yes," Robin said. "And I really think the five of us should be here for Kristen."

Eloise recognized that tone, even if she hadn't heard it in over two decades. This was the take-charge Robin. The one who would not take no for an answer.

The five of us.

Once, the five of them had been Eloise's saving grace. The only place she felt safe, loved.

Eloise sighed as she turned in her chair. "I don't want to come back there," she said. The reason why was a whole new door that Eloise would not let open, not even for a moment.

"Just for a few days," Robin said. "Your dad isn't here anymore, Eloise, and I'm sure your mother would love to see you."

"You should've been a lawyer," Eloise said. Not many people knew Eloise's number one reason for leaving and staying away from Five Island Cove was her father. The door in her mind started to inch open, and Eloise shoved mightily against it. Only a few people knew what life had been like behind the closed doors of the beach cottage where Eloise had grown up with her parents and brother. Garrett had left the islands almost as quickly as Eloise had, and she twisted the key on the lock on that door in her mind.

"And Wes hasn't stepped foot on the island since your divorce." Robin was one of those people who knew the finer details of Eloise's life, a fact she really wished wasn't true right now. At the same time, Eloise thought someone should know the finer details of her life, and while she had friends on campus and neighbors on her street, no one truly knew her the way Robin did.

Point two taken. Eloise really had no reason not to go. "I have some work—"

"The semester ended today," Robin interrupted. "So you're probably sitting at home, finishing up your grades and wondering what you're going to do with all your free time."

"I am not sitting at home," Eloise said, looking at the final class's worth of grades. "And I have plenty to keep me busy." Knitting, and her cats, and...

Suddenly a couple of weeks on Five Island Cove didn't sound so bad. At least she wouldn't have to say she had no plans for her break should someone ask her on her way out of the building that afternoon.

"You could stay with me," Robin said. "I know you don't like going back to your mom's place."

A third blow to Eloise's flimsy tower of excuses sent

it shattering. She drew in a long breath to make a big show. "I don't know, Robin."

"Please," the woman said next, and Eloise's defenses dropped.

"You don't play fair," she said.

"Kristen needs us," Robin said. "And if that means I have to play dirty to get everyone here, I'm going to do it."

"You've talked to AJ?"

"Not yet," Robin hedged.

"You called me first, didn't you?"

"Kristen needs us," she repeated, which was code for *You're a softie. I knew I could get you, and that will help get the others.*

"Fine," Eloise said. "But I'm bringing both of my cats, so you better have somewhere for them too."

"I can handle two felines," Robin said coolly. A moment later, a shriek came through the phone, and Eloise should've known it would sound. But she'd forgotten Robin's tendency to scream in excitement, and she startled, her heart pounding furiously now.

"Oh, I'm so excited, Eloise. We can go to Mort's like we did growing up. And I'll make the chocolate chip banana pancakes that won the fireman's cook-off, and we'll go to the beach and talk about everything."

Everything.

The word inspired fear in Eloise's heart, because she didn't want to talk about everything. Some things, in her opinion, *shouldn't* be talked about. Some secrets were worth keeping. "I need to finish my grades," she said. "And look at flights. I'll text you, okay?"

"I knew you were doing grades," Robin teased.

Eloise managed to smile. "Yeah, but I'm not doing them at home."

"I know," Robin said. "I called you at the university." The pure triumph in Robin's voice wasn't lost on Eloise.

She rolled her eyes, though she did love Robin. "I'll talk to you later." She hung up and stared at her laptop, that last class taunting her now. She acted like she would be really put out with a return visit to Five Island Cove, but maybe it was time. Maybe she could finally put to rest the simmering secrets that she kept in the beach house not even Robin knew about.

Maybe a bit of excitement bubbled through her too. She didn't have any plans for her break, though she had been looking forward to attending her power yoga classes at a more sane hour. And that was when she realized her life had been reduced to knitting, cats, and a half an hour of power yoga at five a.m.

Maybe she could just look at airplane tickets for a few minutes before she finished her grades...

Use your phone to scan the code below to read THE LIGHTHOUSE now!

THE SOUND OF THE SEA

Books in the Five Island Cove series

The Lighthouse, Book 1: As these 5 best friends work together to find the truth, they learn to let go of what doesn't matter and cling to what does: faith, family, and most of all, friendship.

Secrets, safety, and sisterhood...it all happens at the lighthouse on Five Island Cove.

The Summer Sand Pact, Book 2: These five best friends made a Summer Sand Pact as teens and have only kept it once or twice—until they reunite decades later and renew their agreement to meet in Five Island Cove every summer.

Books in the Five Island Cove series

The Cliffside Inn, Book 3: Spend another month in Five Island Cove and experience an amazing adventure between five best friends, the challenges they face, the secrets threatening to come between them, and their undying support of each other.

Christmas at the Cove, Book 4:

Secrets are never discovered during the holidays, right? That's what these five best friends are banking on as they gather once again to Five Island Cove for what they hope will be a Christmas to remember.

Books in the Five Island Cove series

The House on Seabreeze Shore, Book 5: Your next trip to Five Island Cove...this time to face a fresh future and leave all the secrets and fears in the past. Join best friends, old and new, as they learn about themselves, strengthen their bonds of friendship, and learn what it truly means to thrive.

Four Weddings and a Baby, Book 6: When disaster strikes, whose wedding will be postponed? Whose dreams will be underwater?

And there's a baby coming too... Best friends, old and new, must learn to work together to clean up after a natural disaster that leaves bouquets and altars, bassinets and baby blankets, in a soggy heap.

Books in the Five Island Cove series

The Seafaring Girls, Book 7: Journey to Five Island Cove for a roaring good time with friends old and new, their sons and daughters, and all their new husbands as they navigate the heartaches and celebrations of life and love.

But when someone returns to the Cove that no one ever expected to see again, old wounds open just as they'd started to heal. This group of women will be tested again, both on land and at sea, just as they once were as teens.

Rebuilding Friendship Inn, Book 8: Clara Tanner has lost it all. Her husband is accused in one of the biggest heists on the East Coast, and she relocates her family to Five Island Cove–the hometown she hates.

Clara needs all of their help and support in order to rebuild Friendship Inn, and as all the women pitch in, there's so much more getting fixed up, put in place, and restored.

Then a single phone call changes everything.

Will these women in Five Island Cove rally around one another as they've been doing? Or will this finally be the thing that breaks them?

Books in the Five Island Cove series

The Glass Dolphin, Book 9: With new friends in Five Island Cove, has the group grown too big? Is there room for all the different personalities, their problems, and their expanding population?

Books in the Nantucket Point series

The Cottage on Nantucket, Book 1: When two sisters arrive at the cottage on Nantucket after their mother's death, they begin down a road filled with the ghosts of their past. And when Tessa finds a final letter addressed only to her in a locked desk drawer, the two sisters will uncover secret after secret that exposes them to danger at their Nantucket cottage.

The Lighthouse Inn, Book 2: The Nantucket Historical Society pairs two women together to begin running a defunct inn, not knowing that they're bitter enemies. When they come face-to-face, Julia and Madelynne are horrified and dumbstruck—and bound together by their future commitment and their obstacles in their pasts...

Books in the Nantucket Point series

The Seashell Promise, Book 3: When two sisters arrive at the cottage on Nantucket after their mother's death, they begin down a road filled with the ghosts of their past. And when Tessa finds a final letter addressed only to her in a locked desk drawer, the two sisters will uncover secret after secret that exposes them to danger at their Nantucket cottage.

About Jessie

Jessie Newton is a saleswoman during the day and escapes into romance and women's fiction in the evening, usually with a cat and a cup of tea nearby. The Lighthouse is her first women's fiction novel, but she writes as Elana Johnson and Liz Isaacson as well, with over 200 books to all of her names. Find out more at www.feelgoodfictionbooks.com.

Manufactured by Amazon.ca
Acheson, AB